Heart on Fire

First published in USA by Naiad Press in 1996
This edition first published in Great Britain 1997 by
Silver Moon Books, 68 Charing Cross Road,
London WC2H 0BB

Printed in Great Britain by
The Guernsey Press Co. Ltd, Guernsey, C.I.

ISBN 1 872642 454

A CIP catalogue record for this title is available from
the British Library

Silver Moon Books, London
& Silver Moon Books of Leeds
are in no way connected

Heart on Fire

Diana Simmonds

SMB

DEDICATION

This book is a clear case of "without whom" – and is dedicated to

ORH, without whom it wouldn't exist.

To NJW, without whom it would have sagged in the middle.

To CCC, without whom it would be full of people thinking to themselves.

My heartfelt appreciation and gratitude.

ACKNOWLEDGEMENTS

Mike Dogg, Lucy Henstridge and Lizzie Bennett for constant support. Margaret Connolly for constant encouragement. Barbara Grier for reasonably constant sense of humour.

CHAPTER ONE

The landscape beyond the huge tinted windows of the air-conditioned bus shimmered in the sun; reverberant sweeps of red and ocher earth and silvery-gray desert vegetation rolled out as far as the eye could see. It was late spring in the Australian outback and the country was still patchworked with masses of jewel-like wildflowers. From time to time groups of tall dusty-gray kangaroos or high-stepping skittish emus would be startled into stampeding away through the scrub. Yet mostly, the landscape glittered,unmoving and undisturbed. It was a fascinating sight — for anyone who might be looking — but beyond the rough verges of the highway, the human presence was entirely absent, the wilderness untrammeled.

On board the bus all was quiet; inset into the roof above the driver's head, a television screen flickered with the faces of a famous sitcom duo, but the sound had long ago been turned down and nobody was watching. In a seat just behind the driver a big, red-faced man dressed in one of the most lurid Hawaiian shirts imaginable was tapping alternately at the keys of a pocket calculator and at a tiny notebook computer. He was Ed Donlan, manager of the Jody Johnson Band.

Behind him, sprawled in snoring and open-mouthed splendor in their airline-style reclining seats, surrounded by the detritus of long-distance travel — playing cards, guitars, CDs and personal disc players, magazines, drink cans, the remains of pizzas and sandwiches — lay the various members of the Jody Johnson Band.

Red Douglas, lead guitarist and self-appointed sex symbol, lay with his thumbs tucked in his belt and an unattractive patch of dribble on his tight black T-shirt. Ben Dunn, monosyllabic, chess-player and drummer, was curled up in an almost fetal position that unwittingly revealed his permanent state of satisfied gloom. Levine Brown, steel guitar and fiddle player and computer whiz, was as relaxed as Ben was not, while Darren Juneau, bass player and harmony singer, had a permanent smile on his lips, even in deep sleep, that made him the sunniest of the group. With their unalterable three-day stubble, scuffed cowboy boots and extravagant clothes, they could be taken for nothing else but musicians.

Behind them, one sleeping, the other filling in diagrams in a puzzle book, were Jeff, the pale-skinned night owl sound engineer, and Paolo, a muscular and unflappable Australian roadie. At the back of the bus, swaying on racks, was a collection of heavily embroidered classic Western-style stage shirts — three sets of four, all in different colors: rich red, deep blue and sunflower yellow. Beneath the racks was a pile of neatly folded and freshly laundered blue jeans and beside them, on a rack, four pairs of black cowboy boots. Hanging separately, shrouded in plastic wrap, were three full outfits of shirt and pants: all black, encrusted with jet beads and the initials "JJ" picked out in seed pearls. The Jody Johnson Band was no grunge outfit.

Across the aisle, symbolically as well as physically separated from the others by both the narrow space and a tangible sense of detachment and authority, was the band's reason for existence: Jody Johnson. On the seat in front of her lay a gleaming, deep-bodied, blond wood acoustic guitar with the initials "JJ" inlaid in ornate and old-fashioned mother-of-pearl between chromed pegs at the head of its narrow neck. On the floor beside her seat was a half-empty plastic spring water bottle, a jumble of books and magazines and a thick, loose-leaf notebook with two green pens stuck in its spiral binding.

There was also a pile of newspapers where, on the front page of each, Jody's laughing face, angularly beautiful beneath tousled long fair hair, stared out beneath or beside headlines which were all a varia-

3

tion on the theme, "Yes, I'm gay." Then followed stories which echoed the biggest metropolitan daily as it began, "Rising queen of the new country music, Jody Johnson, told a press conference in Sydney today that yes, she is gay. Asked why she had chosen to 'come out' in Australia, Johnson, 30, brought the house down when she said to reporters, 'You guys asked me. It's no big secret. You guys're just more polite. You asked me before you went ahead and wrote your stories. If you ask me a question, most times I'll tell you an answer.' " The story went on: "Jody and her band are in Australia to play an unusual outback tour that will be filmed. Asked why they had picked Australia, Jody said, 'cos nobody else has done it yet.' It is believed that the one-hour documentary for U.S. cable television has been sold to an Australian network."

After anxiously scanning each paper on the flight from Sydney to Adelaide, Ed Donlan had breathed a sigh of relief and turned to Jody with a grin topped by a nervously sweaty upper lip. "Well Jody, I reckon you did the right thing. I know I argued with you, but this has turned out real good. These Aussies seem to like you even more than before. We couldn't have paid for publicity like this. Well done, girl."

Jody frowned and said sharply, "Well done, nothing. I didn't do any favors, Ed, I did it for me. I'm sick and tired of the rumors and whispering. It's nobody's damn business. But now they all know and that will make it boring. So maybe now I can just get on with being a musician."

Ed patted her arm placatingly and said, "Sure, Jody, sure." But the attentiveness that he observed toward Jody's every need, real and imagined, of the

4

cabin staff on the plane — especially the women — made it plain to him that not only was she irrevocably more than "just a musician" in the eyes of the curious public, but that his investment in the Jody Johnson Band was still a safe one, and because of the risk she had insisted on taking — which had given him even more unpleasant trans-Pacific flight indigestion than usual — it was an investment that was likely to yield the kind of return he had only dreamed of throughout his up-and-down career.

This trip to Australia, on the back of a year-old good, top-selling album, had been, in Ed's eyes, the one to hone and toughen the band's increasingly sophisticated concert program in preparation for a grueling three-month big-time-or-bust tour of the American circuit. He also hoped that, with the film, it would consolidate Jody's position as a major star in the making. He had spent twelve hours a day, week in and week out, in his tiny Los Angeles office surrounded by his electronic staff of fax machine and computer, negotiating and confirming the complex trip across the continent demanded by the needs of the concert promoters and the film. He had finally booked the bus for the outback trip and, with the last phase of the tour locked into place, he had crossed his fingers and silently sent up a sheepish little prayer that next time it would be five-star, first class and jet planes all the way.

When Jody insisted that the entire band should travel together on the week-long outback tour, Ed protested that it was not necessary, that he and Jody could afford to fly between film locations and concert dates. But Jody remained immovable, particularly about the trip into the interior that was supposed to be part acclimatization and part regrouping after they had all been scattered on different personal projects for the best part of eight months.

"We've always been together, Ed, it's what keeps the band solid. If you want to hire us a private jet for the next tour then you better start working on the dates and percentages. And you better make sure I've got the studio and the engineers I want for the recording — or there won't be a next tour." And, as in most things in the past six years, Ed had to admit that Jody was probably right. He looked up from his calculations — extra ticket sales had flooded in after the press conference — and checked on his little brood.

Unlike the men, Jody was not asleep but stared out at the passing landscape, drinking in its foreignness — the trees, colors and shapes that were so unlike anything from her childhood in deeply forested and mountainous Washington state. To Ed's practiced gaze she looked rested and at ease, but the firm set of her mouth and the far-away sadness in her eyes pained him. He knew, better than most, the cost in loneliness and an empty personal life of an existence such as this one. Unlike the boys, she was not inclined to take up offers of one-night comfort on the road and, in the years that she and Ed had been building the band for the big time, there had been few lovers willing or able to take second place and to stay quietly at home while Jody disappeared, sometimes for weeks at a time. Ed frequently thanked his lucky stars for the miracle that Jody seemed reconciled to her solitary existence and did not turn to the usual crutches of the musician's life. More than that, she had insisted on making it a condition of each man's contract that drugs were banned and, aside from post-gig beer and bourbon, that's how it was.

Jody seemed to sense his gaze, or maybe she heard his sigh above the all-pervasive drone of the bus's diesel engine. She looked across at him and her eyebrows crinkled into a question mark. Ed shook his head and grinned and, as she grinned back, his heart did a somersault as it often did when taken by surprise by the searchlight warmth of her too-rare smile. He stood up and carefully lurched his way back to her seat and leaned over to speak close to her ear.

"Bookings are way up. We could do some extra dates."

Jody grimaced. "Where?"

"Sydney, Brisbane and Melbourne. Maybe Perth if there's time."

"Is it worth it?"

"I'm working on it." He gestured at the portable empire of electronic gadgetry. "It would be good business — extra shows always build a bit of a buzz."

"Sure." Jody sighed and stretched her long legs. "But this is a heavy schedule already, Ed, especially with this pesky film. And I gotta write some songs before we head back to L.A."

He patted her shoulder reassuringly. "We don't have to make any decisions for a few days, honey. We just need to get this bit over with."

"Yeah, and remind me again why we're heading into the back of beyond? Jeez, Ed, we must be a million miles from somewhere."

Ed chuckled. "Farm Aid. Charity. Big rodeo. You got some stuff from them back in December and you

7

absolutely insisted we fit it in. I told you it was a big hike, but you insisted. Meanwhile, the film company liked the idea too. So here we are."

Jody groaned and rolled her eyes. "But you're the manager, why didn't you manage to tell me we'd have to drive for two years to get to wherever it is?"

"You said, and I quote, 'We oughta see the Outback if we have the chance, Ed. And those farming people,' I quote, 'could do with a good time and some help and they've asked us specially.' End quote."

"How come you can remember things like that when you can't remember when I ask you something really important?"

"Like?"

"Like, I can't remember — that's why I ask you to remember the things that are really important!" Jody emphasized each point with an affectionate punch on the knee.

"Sure, honey, sure. That's why we're heading for the Farm Aid Rodeo in Nowheresville, Outback Australia, the World, the Universe, Space."

Before either could think of further bantering accusations to hurl at each other there was a muffled bang from somewhere deep within the bus's insides. Ed was momentarily thrown off balance as the huge vehicle careened crazily from one side of the bitumen to the other and then, with an almighty lurch, its engine picked up again, but it had gained an ominous and unpleasant noise, like a cement mixer full of rocks.

"What the hell is going on, Andy?" chorused the roughly roused members of the band.

The driver was frantically checking the dials in

front of him while listening to the sound of the afflicted engine. "I dunno!" he yelled back. "But it doesn't sound healthy." He picked up a road map from the console beside him and for a minute divided his attention between it and the road ahead. "Hey, boss," he called to Ed, "we're within an hour of Davanzo's Roadhouse, at Barralong Creek. They have a workshop there and I think we'll have to stop and see what's going on. I don't fancy pushing on any farther with the old girl sounding like this."

Ed sighed, glancing back at the apprehensive faces of his flock. "Okay, Andy, but what's at this joint? Can we get something to eat?" He stared doubtfully at the empty blue-gray strip of road ahead.

"Absolutely, boss. Davanzo's is one of the world's best truckstops. Great tucker — I mean, food — and pretty nice people. We'll be fine."

"Well, I guess we don't have much choice. You're in charge of Ol' Tammy's innards."

Andy laughed. "I don't know that Miss Wynette would appreciate that, mate."

Ed grinned. "You're right, just as well she doesn't know that we honored her this way." He turned to the group, whose anxious faces were all turned to him. "Attention please, ladies and gentlemen," Ed said in his best airline pilot's voice. "We are going to make a short unscheduled stop at um . . . some creek or other, where we will take in the sights, grab a bite to eat and let Andy here have a fiddle with Ol' Tammy and see what ails her. All those in favor please let me have your boarding passes before disembarkation. Thank you." He tried to ignore the chorus of groans and balled up bits of paper that came flying through the air. "Andy tells me this place is famous for its food and I am sure you will find it much more welcoming than what's out there." He waved his hand at the empty landscape beyond the windows. "Any further questions?"

The mutters and mock snarls that were his answer allowed him to sit down and pretend to resume his previous tapping onto the notebook computer's keyboard, but in reality his heart had sunk into his boots. He glanced back at Jody but her face was impassive and she seemed to find the view even more fascinating than she had before. He knew that if there was trouble, she would be the one whose stoicism, good humor and calm acceptance of fate — in the form of missed planes, blown electrical circuits or sickly tour buses — would help him through the tantrums and arguments generated by the enforced captivity of a bunch of highly strung, egotistical young men.

Sometimes, he knew, Jody's cool exterior was almost unhealthy. It was as if she was resigned rather than accepting of circumstances, her emotions unreachable. Often, he thought, she seemed to withdraw so completely it could only be the reaction of a wounded creature — unwilling to endure more pain and able to fall back on unseen and unplumbed depths to do so. His mind flicked back to the early morning departure from Adelaide when the newspapers had been gathered and fallen upon by the band members. Red Douglas, raucous, extroverted and — Ed long suspected — unconsciously jealous of Jody's effortless effect on women, had read out bits of the stories, mimicking a pompous newsreader-style voice, unaware of Jody's frozen acceptance of the moment and the probability that he was carelessly humiliating her more than anything that had been splashed across the front pages.

Now, she was once again a remote but calm presence, knees drawn up to her chin, hands loosely clasped around her ankles as she refused to be drawn into the waves of anxiety and bickering that ebbed and flowed around the rest of the group. But finally, when she pointed out a group of leaping gray kangaroos, she succeeded in diffusing the mood completely and even joined in the laughter as Darren Juneau, with his nose in the air, eyes half-closed and hands clasped high in front of his chin, began a quite accurate pantomime of the animals, up and down the aisle. By the time Andy called out, "Take your seats, we're coming in to land!" the atmosphere had lifted and been restored. They all sat forward eagerly and examined the remote refuge that was looming large in Ol' Tammy's dusty windshield.

The truckstop on the northbound highway had been known as Davanzo's for as long as any professional trucker could remember because of the roadhouse and motel cabins that had been there for some forty years. Run by the same family for all that time, the management was into its second generation with Margaret and Tony Davanzo in charge, Tony's mother Iris still very much a part of the place and her husband Alphonso buried on the hill out back.

Working down through the gears, Andy pulled the big bus slowly off the bitumen and cruised at almost walking pace into the shade of a stand of tall, graceful eucalypti before gently applying the brakes.

Jody realized, as she looked about, that his careful exit from the highway had kept the swirl of red dust kicked up in their wake to the minimum. A smile flickered across her face as she caught his eye in the rearview mirror and she gave him a double thumbs' up. To her amusement she saw a blush darken the leathery ruddy tan of his neck and face and he grinned, sheepishly.

Jody hung back and let the men get off first. Beyond the high curved corrugated metal roof that sheltered the fuel bowsers, the roadhouse stood, a long, low, two-story wood and corrugated iron building, surrounded by a deep wooden veranda over which grew honeysuckle and a massive magenta bougainvillea. Behind that, Jody could see what looked like motel cabins clustered in the shade of old pepper trees by the wide winding bed of a creek, beside which were a half dozen rustic picnic tables and benches and some rough stone barbecue fireplaces.

The musicians took in nothing of this. They tumbled down the steps in extravagantly rowdy fashion, playing, she knew, at being outrageous musicians. It was harmless enough but more often than not, Jody did not have the energy or inclination to put into such a performance. Nevertheless, she grinned to herself, there was an image to keep up. She reached under her seat for her fawn "number two" hat, made sure the new pale pink Australian parrot feathers — scavenged from the parklands across from the Adelaide hotel — were in place in the woven band, twisted her hair into a rope on top of her head and settled the hat over it before ambling down the steps and breathing in her first surprising taste of thick, hot, dusty Outback air.

By the time she reached the doors of the roadhouse — topped by a red swirl of curly neon lettering announcing "Davanzo's" — Jody could feel sweat prickling the skin between her shoulder blades. Ben was standing in the doorway, wiping his face on his shirt sleeve and frowning. "This is supposed to be spring?" he said, his voice heavy with disbelief and disgruntlement.

Jody grinned and squeezed his shoulder. "Sure as hell beats freezing your fingers in Oklahoma in February," she said, and slipped ahead of him. "C'mon, drummer man, I'll buy you a glass of something liquid."

Inside she stopped abruptly. The building was unexpectedly cool and almost dim after the heat and brilliant sunlight outside — the veranda and angled wooden blinds made sure of that. They were no match for the noise level, however, which was also several notches higher than she had expected. She quickly saw that the pandemonium was coming from tables where a group of truck drivers and the men of the Johnson Band were in the middle of what was, to Jody, the now-familiar mutual admiration and male bonding ritual of long distance truck drivers and country musicians. It involved autographing virtually anything that could be written on while laughing, joking and slapping backs as loudly and as boisterously as possible. A few other customers — intrepid RV campers and backpackers by the look of their variously folksy "travel" wear — looked on with interest and bemusement. Behind the counter, in red and white checked aprons embroidered with their names on the bib pockets, stood two people who seemed to be the proprietor and his wife, Tony and Margaret Davanzo, a handsome, silver-haired couple looking at once vaguely surprised but tolerant at the unexpected invasion of their establishment.

When Red noticed Jody and Ben standing in the doorway he let out a whoop and yell of "Jo-dee!" which meant that any trucker hitherto unaware of who she was now demanded her attention. In the thick of the melee Ed turned pleading eyes in her direction and Jody grinned and sauntered over in her best laid-back country gal sashay. It was, she knew, disconcerting for those who may have thought they had her pegged as a man-hater and toughie to see her move like a model on a catwalk. Particularly as they were unlikely to be aware that her jeans and shirt, while faded and worn, had not been pulled off a supermarket peg but rather, especially and carefully tailored to emphasize her long legs, hips, neat waist and full breasts.

"It's not vanity," she had once said to Ed when he accused her, in their penny-pinching early days, of extravagance, "but I do know how to display the goods and, let's face it, *I am* the goods we're selling." She had been so matter-of-fact about it that he had decided, then and there, that this time he was in for the long haul. This one was going all the way.

He was reminded, in a flash, of that long-ago moment as Jody slid into the center of the group and began dispensing easy charm, funny remarks and autographs much as a market trader would sell choice fruit. As Jody went about her business of generally being "one of the boys," Ed unobtrusively extricated himself and slid over to the counter to introduce himself, arrange help for Andy and the bus and a supply of food and drink for the tribe.

Accustomed as he was to expecting any kind of reception, from downright hostile to smotheringly effusive, Ed was pleasantly surprised to have his hand shaken warmly as Margaret and Tony welcomed him and the band with the assurance that the Jody Johnson Band CD was one of the most popular on the jukebox. Then, as the two halves of the kitchen doors parted, Tony beckoned to the tall, dark-haired woman who peered out, frowning at the racket.

"Mr. Ed, this is my daughter, Graziella," Tony said, proudly. "Come and meet Mr. Ed." He waved his arm expansively at the room in general. "He is the manager of the Jody Johnson Band."

"Ed, ma'am, just plain Ed," said Ed, bowing slightly as he found himself being appraised by the coolest, darkest and deepest pair of eyes he could ever recall having seen.

"I'm glad to meet you, Ed," she said in a voice as cool and dark as her eyes. "Everybody but my father calls me Grace, so please do."

"She is our pride and joy," said Tony Davanzo, beaming at his daughter even as she sent him a look that could have skewered a kebab. "She is a university fine arts graduate and she is building a name for herself as a painter and illustrator of our native flora and fauna."

"Papa! Please!" Grace protested, laughing at her father's unabashed pride.

Margaret Davanzo slapped at her husband with an order pad. "You talk too much, old man," she joked. "Grace, my darling, we have some very hungry boys for lunch." She turned to Ed. "How about we get you my special meatballs in tomato sauce, some big bowls of pasta and some good bread and fresh salad and fruit?"

"That sounds just about perfect, ma'am," said Jody's voice from behind Ed. She had slipped away from the tangled knot of men and leaned on the counter, her widest smile in place. "This must be heaven but we just didn't know we died yet."

As the laughter subsided Jody realized that from her vantage point behind the high glassed-in part of the counter that held an array of hot snacks, Grace had not joined in but was looking on with ill-concealed distaste. She was clearly aghast at the crude manners of the members of the band — typical rock musicians, Jody could almost see her thinking — and obviously, as far as she was concerned, their leader was in the thick of it.

But Tony and Margaret didn't notice the exchange of chilly stares between them. Clearly they were thrilled to have Jody under their roof, and clearly, Grace was surprised as it became apparent that they were big fans. Margaret listed her favorite songs on the CD. Then it was Jody's turn to be surprised when Margaret went back over three previous albums, two of which, to Jody's certain knowledge, had never reached a wide public. It was a toss-up as to who was more amazed — Jody or Grace.

"I thought you only ever listened to opera, Papa?" Grace said. "What happened to Callas and Tebaldi?"

"I think this girl has been away from home too long and in that university too long," said Tony, hugging his daughter so fondly that no element of criticism remained in his remark.

"For once your father is right," said Margaret, "You don't understand, Grace. Jody, she sings like an angel — she could be Italian!"

Jody laughed uproariously and slapped the counter, playing up — she realized ruefully — to Grace's image of her as the hayseed country singer.

"You are too young to remember Connie Francis!" Margaret went on, speaking to Jody. "But you have a voice that reminds me of her. Only better."

Jody took off her hat, stuck out her hand to Margaret, and this time she was not play-acting. "I take that as a compliment, ma'am," she said softly and was only slightly taken aback when Margaret leaned over the counter and kissed her firmly on both cheeks. Then, clearly determined not to be left out, Tony took her free hand and kissed it with a great flourish.

In sheer wickedness Jody glanced at Grace, winked and raised her eyebrows, as if to say "See! You can't get me now!" And Grace could not help but grin and grimace despairingly.

"Okay, you win," she said to Jody, a statement that clearly puzzled her parents and Ed; then she added, "Now I've got to do something about your lunch, if you'll all excuse me."

* * * * *

17

In the swirl of good-natured coming and going around the restaurant, only Ed noticed that Jody was not the only one to keenly watch Grace until she disappeared through the kitchen doors; Red Douglas's antenna had immediately homed in on the presence of a beautiful woman and, despite continuing a bantering conversation with Levine Brown and a bearded truck driver, his pale blue eyes had taken in Grace's every aspect. Ed could not tell whether the flutter deep in the pit of his stomach was simply apprehension or something else more pleasant as he considered the possibilities.

CHAPTER TWO

Back once again in the comparative haven of the kitchen Grace took a deep breath and leaned against the chilly metal door of the cool room. Even though she was twenty-eight and married and divorced, she could not persuade her father to be anything but as proud and adoring of his only daughter as he had been when she first went off to school with a clean white handkerchief in her pocket. She had been made to realize, yet again, that there were things about her parents that had escaped her notice in the years since she left home. She appreciated how generous and wise in their outlook they were on most things — that there had never been a word of criticism or doubt when she left her husband and returned home with her heart and body bruised and her tail between her legs. But, she thought wryly, they never ceased to amaze her nevertheless, and she couldn't help but wonder whether they had seen the morning's newspapers, plastered as they were with pictures and the sensational story of their new favorite guest.

What on earth, she wondered, would they make of Jody Johnson's blatantly admitted sexuality? What on earth did she — nicely brought up Grace Davanzo — make of it? she asked herself. Jody's grin and twinkling teasing eyes flashed across her mind, and she had an instant of perfect recall of how Jody's hair looked, dropping in a shaggy, honey-colored swathe onto her shoulders when she'd pulled off her hat. And she also — she realized with relief — could recall the appreciative slow burn in Red's blue eyes and the sensuousness of his smile as he had slowly and deliberately looked her up, down and all the way back up again. The flare of heat between her legs and the sudden hard thumping of her heart gave Grace a jolt for which she was unprepared. Good heavens, she thought, a year without a man and I'm ready for anything. But, she chided herself, that was a flippant thought and as likely as a frosty Sunday in summer . . .

"Grace! What are you day-dreaming about!" Her mother's face was framed comically by the swinging doors. "We need meatballs to feed an army out here. Do you want me to give you a hand?"

Guiltily Grace leapt away from the cooling comfort

of the metal and wiped her hands on her apron. "Sorry! Give me five minutes and you'll have meatballs coming out of your ears."

"Into their mouths will be enough, my darling."

Grace went to tend the pot of fresh tomato sauce and so did not see the warily speculative but loving look in Margaret's eyes — one that lingered long after she had withdrawn her head from the doorway and disappeared back into the restaurant.

Within half an hour the food was ready. It was not often that Grace could be persuaded out of the kitchen. Dealing with customers, she told her parents, was not what she was good at. She was naturally reserved and the years away had made it even more difficult for her to adopt the easy-going jocularity that went down well with their customers. But, when the trays loaded with bowls of steaming, garlicky-spicy, sauce-rich meatballs were ready for the band, Grace amazed herself as much as her mother when she slipped the ties of her apron, ran her fingers through her curly crop of mahogany-colored hair and prepared to deliver the food to their tables.

As she looked around the room she saw that Jody had not returned to the raucous group of men and was perched on a stool at the counter, turning on a completely beguiling and gentle smile as Margaret and Tony, it seemed from the fragments she caught, told her the entire life history of the Davanzo clan.

"Quite a performer," Grace thought grouchily. It was clear that Margaret and Jody were already as good as old friends — and, she was dumbfounded to realize, there sat her crusty grandmother — Iris. The old woman had been tempted away from her hide- away in the back room where she cursed and hated, but always watched, the midday TV chat shows. Now, Grace saw, she was laughing uproariously at something Jody had leaned toward her and quietly said.

Grace frowned in concentration as she carried trays of plates to the two tables which the band had immediately made their territory. The sighs and whoops of delight as they sniffed the aroma rising from the bowls were, Grace thought, boyish and rather sweet — not as nerve-wracking as she had expected. With Jenny, the regular waitress, handing out thick white china dishes and no-nonsense stainless steel cutlery, Grace transferred the food to each table and even managed a couple of jokes and flirtatious banter with the handsome Red. Not that she could remember a word of their exchange; being this out of practice was something she had not considered and it was more intimidating than she had anticipated. With a sigh of relief she escaped back to the area behind the counter from which she could survey the room in comparative safety. Jody made no move to join the band and did not seem to be in a hurry to get away from Davanzo family gossip. She looked completely relaxed, Grace thought, and strangely glamorous and elegant, although she was wearing only a simple pale blue denim shirt and faded jeans. After a moment Grace wondered whether this was "country singer" disguise — the fit of the clothes was snug but not tight and showed off a rangy but well-fleshed body without being spectacularly revealing. The look was finished off with the quintessential Western accessories: a heavy and intricately worked silver and turquoise choker around her neck and high-heeled black boots, dusty and worn to what looked like comfortable perfection.

Nobody deserves legs that long, Grace thought as Jody suddenly turned toward her and smiled with green eyes which somehow combined warmth and a cool assessment. To her absolute irritation, Grace felt herself blushing and, involuntarily, she smiled back with more enthusiasm than she thought she had permitted herself.

"Y'all seem to be mighty friendly 'round here," Jody said in an exaggerated Jimmy Stewart drawl and in a tone of dark melted chocolate that seemed to be aimed, Grace felt, directly and sardonically at her. "Could a person be gettin' a cup of that fine Aussie coffee that comes outta those machines?"

Before Grace could answer or make a move, her mother was at the machine, almost knocking down her husband in her eagerness to get to it, to make what she assured Jody would be "proper espresso." Despite herself, Grace felt a wave of affection and amusement for her mother's total capitulation to this beautiful and, it seemed, charming stranger. And she wondered what other kind of life Margaret might have chosen for herself if she had not married Tony and, with him, the daily grind and isolation of the truckstop.

Back in the kitchen once again, Grace began preparing more food. How do we choose our lives? she wondered, as she rapidly and finely chopped garlic and onions. Was it fate or was that just an excuse? She chose to marry Scott and she chose to leave. At least, it was supposed to be choice. Reluctantly she recalled the way he had pushed his way into her life, taking it over until she found herself swept along into whatever absurd scheme he dreamed up. At first it had been fun, exhilarating after her solidly careful childhood and safely careful school days in the cloistered atmosphere of Catholic boarding school in Adelaide. But then, as the roller coaster of Scott's ideas on how to make money began to go down more often than they had gone up, it gradually ceased to be exciting and had turned into a frightening and finally life-threatening plunge.

Grace nicked the tip of her index finger with the razor-edged steel blade and she stopped chopping and laid down the knife. As always, thinking about Scott and the years of her marriage was producing in her a state of agitation that was as dangerous as it was unpleasant. She took several deep breaths and watched as a bead of almost black blood welled up in the cut. For a moment, even more unwelcome pictures flickered before her eyes: blood dripping from her nose and a gash through her left eyebrow when he had crashed their old car one drunken night. Blood seeping from welts on her back the night he had beaten her for the last time and finally left her for — he had screamed over his shoulder — "someone who's a real woman. Not a ball-breaking bitch like you!" It had been the second last time they had seen one another. The last time had been in a lawyer's office when he had tried in vain to keep her from retaining her own meager belongings.

"Grace, my darling..." Grace jumped as her mother's arm slipped around her waist.

"Ma! You startled me." Grace sucked on her finger and tried to smile, but as always, her mother's dark eyes were too penetrating for pretense. "Just having a little nightmare, Mama. It always happens when I chop onions. It gives me too much time to think." She grinned and kissed her mother on the tip of her olive-skinned, aquiline nose.

Margaret kissed her back. "You have always thought too much about the wrong things," she said and hugged her daughter. "Now we have to think about good things like feeding extra mouths and finding them beds for the night."

"They're staying?"

"They have to. There's something seriously wrong with their gearbox and it can't be fixed without parts from Adelaide. They won't arrive before tomorrow evening. Just as well we're not too busy."

"True. Well, the beds are all freshly made up. Jenny and I did them yesterday. They can just walk straight in."

Margaret gave her another little squeeze. "What will we do when you go, my darling? Your father and I really appreciate everything you have been doing. You know that, don't you?"

"I do, Ma, but I'm not going anywhere. Look at the mess I made last time. And they're not exactly queuing at the door." Grace began chopping onions again, but Margaret stopped her.

"Don't say things like that, Grace. And don't think them either. You are a wonderful, wonderful girl and somebody equally wonderful will happen for you, you wait and see."

Grace grinned and thwacked an onion in half with one blow. "Sure, Mama. Maybe. But I don't know that I'm in the market for anyone, wonderful or not."

"That's when they come along — when you're not in the market. You wait and see. Now, leave those onions alone and please take our guests to their cabins. Your father is up to his ears in grease somewhere in that bus and your grandmother can't be trusted with keys and I —" She pushed back her sleeves, sighed deeply and looked ecstatically happy. "I have to make gnocchi for Jody."

Grace accepted defeat and untied the strings of her apron. "Have you signed them in, Mama?" she asked as she sluiced her face and hands in blissfully cold water.

"Your father did all the paperwork with Mr. Ed. The boys are taking three cabins between them and Jody can have number eight."

Grace nodded and made no comment. Number eight was farthest away from the noise of the road-house and the highway and was also sheltered from the rest of the complex by two old olive trees and a hedge of deep pink hibiscus and oleander. It was the cabin given to visiting friends and relatives, or special guests.

Grace braced herself for more boisterous flirtation and banter and went through the swinging doors to the restaurant. Again it turned out to be more fun than she had anticipated. In their various ways the members of the band were used to making acquaintances quickly and settling themselves into strange situations at the speed of light. Grace took the keys from the board in the office, a pile of rough white towels and, after much bowing and "after you," "no, after you" larking at the door, led them in a knockabout, muck-about troupe out of the air-conditioned comfort of the main building. As they crossed the forecourt, they gasped, groaned and marveled at the heat and brightness of the afternoon sun, while Jody followed at a distance, saying nothing, her hat pulled down inscrutably over her eyes.

In a corner of her mind, Grace realized that she found Jody's detachment slightly irritating. But she was too busy giving back as good as she got from the band members to be able to give it her full attention, which was just as well, she reasoned, because she had enough to deal with without having to consider the sensibilities of guests who thought themselves a cut above the available company and accommodation.

Grace unlocked each door and ceremoniously handed over a key to whichever musician seemed less likely to immediately lose it. "You can eat any time," she told them. "But there's always a daily dinner menu from seven, and tonight's special is Mama's gnocchi with wild mushroom sauce. It's very, very good."

At that bit of news, Grace saw Jody's indifference disappear in a flash. "Wild mushrooms?" she exclaimed. "Where from?"

"Not far from here," Grace said, waving vaguely toward the eastern horizon. "It's a cow paddock and my grandfather seeded it with mushrooms from the old country a long time ago, before I was born, and back they come, every autumn. My grandmother dries them so we can eat them almost all year."

"Well whaddya know," Jody murmured. "And I thought we'd be lucky to find a canned hotdog out here."

"This is Australia, not the Midwest," said Grace

tartly and was rewarded by a chorus of whoops and hollers from the band.

"Hot damn, Jody! I think you just got your ass kicked!" Red Douglas punched the air with his fist, and the expression on Jody's face was a mixture of embarrassment and annoyance. But Darren Juneau burst into a high, fluting comically exaggerated chorus of "I'm Sorry" and the fresh waves of laughter seemed, Grace saw, to diffuse the spark of tension between Jody and Red who turned away to Grace once again.

"What's there to do around these parts, Gracey?" From the confident grin on his face, Red Douglas, the lead guitarist, had clearly decided Grace was the girl for him.

Jody watched him try his charm. He was an attractive, swaggering fellow with a shock of red-gold ringlets and a classically handsome pale-skinned face. He was obviously used to having women falling at his feet. "It's only a matter of time," he'd told her as they had collected their bags from the bus. "Only a matter of time before this truckstop princess is eating out of my hand."

Jody had said nothing in return and now, as Red grinned down at Grace, she still said nothing but stared off into the distance once more and tapped her foot — just firmly enough for the sound to be audible. Red glared at her. "You in a hurry or something, Jody, huh?"

Jody dragged her gaze from the distant blue ridge of hills and frowned slightly, before shaking her head and smiling. "I'm in no hurry, Red," she said softly. "You take your time, son. You'll need all the time you can get."

Red's face flushed to deep pink as the rest of the band rocked with laughter. Even Grace — Jody noticed — grinned, but then she saw Red's fury and the grin disappeared instantly.

"There's not a great deal in the way of socializing as you would recognize it," she said to Red in a voice that Jody recognized to be practiced in the art of soothing ruffled male pride, "but people get together at the roadhouse on Friday nights and there's a film show at the community hall on Saturday nights. If you're here that long . . ." She held out a key to him and after a moment he took it from her, almost gently.

"Then maybe we can get together this evening, Gracey," he said easily. "Have a few beers maybe."

Grace smiled at them all. "I'd like to have a drink with everybody later," she said lightly. "I get off at ten and that's when we generally relax and have a drink and something to eat with friends who may be around — when it's cooler."

Jody did not smile outwardly, but as she looked off again toward the blue hills she was laughing inside. The "truckstop princess" would not be the pushover Red had anticipated. She turned away and examined the rest of the compound, wondering which of the small, tree-shaded cabins had been allocated to her. Suddenly the idea of a cool shower and getting out of her dusty, sweaty clothes was the most important thing in the world, and the stickiness of her skin was immediately close to unbearable. She looked again at Grace, watching her as she handed over keys and instructions to each of the boys. She was a few years younger, Jody figured, and somehow at ease in this extraordinary climate. Maybe it was the Italian genes. And maybe that's my silly prejudice, she told herself.

Nevertheless, there was something in the classic Latin looks — shining dark hair curling in a skull-cap short crop, flawless olive skin and the lushness of the well-proportioned but work-hardened body — that reminded Jody of an old-style Italian film star, Sophia Loren or Gina Lollobrigida, maybe. She tried to remember which one and which film in particular and was staring intently at Grace when the up-turned black cat's eyes caught her own and widened perceptibly at the discovered intensity of the gaze. Disconcerted and more than a little discomfited, Jody smiled awkwardly but Grace did not return it; instead, her chin rose proudly and she turned back to the boys and the ritual handing-out of their keys and towels.

To her own surprise, Jody felt unnerved by the chilly response and found herself thinking that Red was welcome, but that he had better watch out. Grace wasn't anything like his usual style of easy pickup groupie. Jody scuffed the dust into patterns with the toe of her boot as unbidden thoughts entered her mind about her own encounters with women who liked to hang around bands. An extra prickle of sweat trickled down her back at the memory of the last time and she shuddered.

It had been a cold winter's night in Albuquerque and, after the exhilaration of a brilliant concert, Jody had felt an icy loneliness grip her as she sat staring at a TV whose sound had been turned down in the midst of a typically raucous post-gig bash. Red had somehow acquired a pair of peachy ripe young women who looked like cheerleaders who'd wandered into the wrong party. They could have stepped out of a shampoo or toothpaste commercial, so glossy-perfect and gleaming were the attributes that they flashed and tossed with such careful abandon.

They had to be called Sue-Anne and Dee-Anne and they were. Jody was idly rolling bourbon around a glass and wondering how Red intended to juggle them both when the one named Dee-Anne dropped onto the couch beside her. "Can I keep you company?" she asked in a breathy voice that must have taken a lot of practice. Then she slid her hand up Jody's leg, from knee to crotch and, uncharacteristically, Jody thought, oh, what the hell, why not.

The reason "why not" became apparent in the early hours of the morning when Jody was roused from a fitful drowse by what she instantly realized was a camera flash. She opened her eyes to find Dee-Anne kneeling at the foot of the tousled bed, in all her over-ripe golden-breasted nakedness, with a small disposable camera in her hand.

"Hi, Jody, honey!" she said brightly. "You don't mind if I have a li'l souvenir, do you?"

Jody's stomach turned over even as she recalled Dee-Anne's calmly expert tongue probing and sucking her toward a weirdly disoriented orgasm. "Do you think you can blackmail me?" she asked, and Dee-Anne's answer was more depressing than even that possibility.

"Hell, no, honey. I just like to have a li'l

memento. I gotta li'l pocket album — look right here..." She slipped off the bed and scampered across the room to rummage in her bag.

Jody cringed as Dee-Anne happily leafed through the plastic-sheathed pages, pointing out singer after singer and musician after musician with whom the Jody Johnson Band shared, she now realized, much more than space on posters and time on stages. And then she thought, with a blind flash of fear, about the drug habits and sexual boasting of many of the men whose frowzy faces and proudly displayed genitals leapt out of the photographs at her and she felt her stomach begin to heave. She took the camera and headed for the bathroom.

"I think you better leave," she muttered from behind her hand. "Take some money for the camera — on the dresser — and please go." She barely managed to lock the door behind her before violent retching and angry tears began to empty her, over and over, until she finally felt herself completely drained and cold. That had been more than a year ago and the memory still had the power to make her shiver and feel both sad and unclean.

"Are you feeling okay?" Grace's voice, and the hand on her arm, turned the shiver into a gasp and uncontrollable recoil. Grace stood back a pace and raised her hands placatingly. "I'm sorry. I startled you. Are you okay? You look..."

Jody took a deep breath and only just restrained herself from touching the place on her arm where Grace's hand had momentarily lain. "God, I'm sorry," she said. "I was..." She shook her head. How could she explain?

"You were thinking about something you'd rather not think about," Grace said wryly.

They regarded each other for the longest moment and Jody finally nodded. "You're right," she conceded. An involuntary shudder shook her. "Sometimes you don't have to be asleep to have nightmares."

"True," Grace said solemnly. Again she put out her hand and touched Jody's arm, giving it a re-assuring and friendly squeeze. "Well, look at it this way, whatever you were dreaming about, it's a helluva long way from here."

Jody felt a burst of good feeling and laughter well up inside as she looked around at the myriad greens of the eucalypti and the already comforting familiarity of the roadhouse buildings. There were definitely no ghosts or horrors here.

Grace patted her shoulder. "Let me show you your cabin," she said gently. "There are a couple of dozen parrots that visit, but nothing that goes bump in the night. I think you'll be comfortable, and I imagine you'd like a shower and a rest."

Jody bit her tongue on the impulse to say no, she did not want a rest, she wanted to keep talking to this mysterious and unexpected woman, and instead allowed herself to be led across to the farthest reaches of the compound.

Grace unlocked the door of the cabin and led the way inside. "There is air conditioning, if you want it." She pointed to the unit set in the wall. "But we generally find the ventilation works well enough." She grinned disarmingly at Jody. "I think it's much healthier without."

Jody smiled and nodded as she saw how one wall

of the little building was constructed of wooden louvers fronted by fine mesh screens, while in the roof there were more louvers that controlled the flow of air and automatically took out the heat. "This is lovely," she said slowly. "How unusual. Who went to all this trouble?" She gestured at the louver arrangement and the screens.

"If you were here in summer you'd know why the screens are essential," Grace said. "They could carry you away. And my grandfather dreamed up the louvers. I think you could call him an early greenie." She looked out at the bush beyond the compound's edge where the creek bed was visible. "He's buried up there." She pointed toward the distant hazy-blue ridge.

Jody stood beside her and looked up toward the hills. The angle of the cabin effectively cut all sound from the compound and the bush was all that existed. "We could be a million miles from anywhere. It's wonderful."

"I'm glad you like it," said Grace. "A lot of people, especially city people, find it threatening. My ..." She paused for a moment, then swallowed and went on, "My ex-husband hated it."

Jody's grin disguised the unexpected jolt to her heart that Grace's last words had provoked. "I'm not a city girl," she said. "I can't claim this kind of country, but if you could imagine it raining for maybe two hundred days a year, you'd get a picture."

"Where are you from, then?"

"Washington — that's the state, not the capital city — the Pacific Northwest. Home of Jimi Hendrix and Kurt Cobain — and Jody Johnson."

"It must be something in the water." Grace laughed, "There's obviously enough of it."

Jody grinned. "Speaking of water, would you care for a drink?" She heard her voice as if it belonged to someone else and was only aware that she did not want Grace to go — or maybe she didn't want to be alone. Then Grace smiled and she knew it wasn't that — she wanted Grace to stay.

"That's very kind," Grace said, "But I have a lot to do. We're short-handed right now." She moved toward the door. "Why don't you join us for a drink this evening. I know my parents would love it."

Jody nodded and smiled. "Sure, that will be good," she said. But as she stood in the doorway watching Grace walk back toward the roadhouse, she felt herself slide into the familiar pit of loneliness out of which this almost-stranger had unknowingly lifted her. Without thinking, she watched the lithe figure swing fluidly across the yard and up the steps to the kitchen door, where Grace paused and looked back and their eyes met and locked.

Whatever she may have expected, something else happened. Shock registered on Grace's face and Jody felt it too. Simultaneously they each raised one hand and their eyes — darker than dark and greener than blue — and the moment was like a current crackling between them. Then Grace turned and disappeared into the roadhouse and Jody shut her cabin door. But for another minute she stood leaning against it, her heart thumping and her thoughts in disarray. Nothing coherent emerged, then she heard herself say in a voice so quiet she wondered whether she had spoken aloud, "Grace. Grace Davanzo."

It felt good and sounded better. Then she shook herself angrily and marched to the bathroom. "A married woman," she told herself firmly. But her pesky and ever-present inner voice replied, "A divorced woman." Jody pulled her dusty, sweaty shirt off and threw it on the floor. "A divorced straight woman," she told the inner voice. "Oh sure," said the irritating inner voice. "Sure."

CHAPTER THREE

In the kitchen of the roadhouse Grace's own thoughts were in turmoil. A flush spread over the skin at the base of her throat and signified, she knew, extreme agitation. The flood of pleasure she had felt when she had turned to see Jody watching her had been shock enough, but now the confusion was only compounded by her very clear wish to spend more time with Jody. She'd made herself leave the cabin when her only desire had been to stay and take up the proffered invitation to a drink. "Jody was being polite," she told herself fiercely. "Americans are always polite, and I had hung around. She was just being polite." Her body was suffused with heat when she recalled the way Jody looked at her and how she, in turn, could not look away.

On automatic pilot, Grace up-ended a sack of potatoes into the deep steel sink and turned a stream of cold water onto them. It splashed back and showered her face with icy droplets; they were a momentary relief from the inner tumult. There was something about Jody that she found unaccountably disturbing and it wasn't, she knew after a minute's careful consideration, simply because she was the first famous lesbian she had ever met. She picked up a small brush and began scrubbing at the potatoes, not grumbling to herself — for once — about why on earth her mother insisted on them rather than the pre-cut variety. After a while, the methodical movement and cold water had a meditative effect and her thoughts began to crystallize and become clearer.

She could remember this sense of deep disturbance happening to her only once before, and it had been when she first met Scott. He had been a powerful and charismatic presence and she had felt herself drawn almost unwillingly toward him and trapped, like a rabbit in a spotlight. Her attraction to him had been intense and his domination had been exciting, at first — utterly different than anything she had experienced in a lifetime of gentle father and gentle grandfather and potent matriarchs. Was there any way, she had asked herself a thousand times, that she should have seen how that power could so easily be abused? Why had she been unable to see through the charm and charisma to the dark heart of the man?

And now, she thought, scrubbing frantically at a hapless potato, how could it be that Jody triggered that same sense of upheaval? A clattering tray broke into her thoughts and Grace turned, relieved, to see who had entered the kitchen. It was her mother. "Are our unexpected guests settled in, my darling?"

Grace nodded, wiping her forehead with the back of her hand. "All happy, I think, Ma," she said. "And I've washed enough potatoes to make gnocchi for the whole of South Australia." She dried her hands on her jeans and stretched her shoulders.

"Thank you, my darling. You are the very best potato washer I've ever known, and don't let anyone ever tell you otherwise." They rubbed noses and laughed. "Does Jody like the back cabin?"

"She does. I think she was pretty impressed with it, actually."

"That's good. I thought she would appreciate it. She is a most interesting young woman." Grace said nothing. "Don't you think, my darling?"

Grace nodded. "She seems very nice," she said limply, and wondered what she meant by that.

"I have been trying to think who she reminds me of," Margaret said as she busied herself gathering the necessities for gnocchi making. "It was just in the back of my mind and I couldn't think. Then I said to your father, 'That Jody, she reminds me of somebody,' and he said it — just like that." She snapped her fingers. "He said, 'She could be Scott's sister. They are very alike, it's the hair,' and I realized he was right, but of course it's also the coloring. When you think about it, they're not a bit alike really, but the coloring and maybe her nose — you get a flash of what he might have looked like if he'd been a girl.

39

Or if he had a sister." She paused in her bustling and looked at Grace who was hanging onto the edge of the steel sink with both hands. "What do you think, my darling? Do you see it? Only a certain physical likeness, of course. She is not a bit like him otherwise, I'm sure."

Grace said nothing for a moment as the shock waves crashed around her head and heart. Why she had not noticed the resemblance before, she could only hazard a guess, along the lines of how very hard she strove, every day, to put Scott out of her conscious mind. But of course, it was obvious — the thick, rich blond hair, the hawklike cheekbones and aquiline nose, the rangy frame and distant but magnetic aura that seemed to say, "Leave me alone," even as it drew attention. She nodded slowly. "You're right," she said, her voice faint in her own ears. "I hadn't seen it, but you're right." She turned to her mother who frowned and came to her quickly.

"My darling," she said, taking her daughter in her arms. "You look as if you've seen a ghost." She hugged Grace and stroked her curly hair gently. "He is gone, my darling. Long gone. And all that is over and this Jody — it's not her fault that she has beautiful hair like pouring honey and a face like an Egyptian statue! We must not be unkind to her because she does not look like the back of that broken-down old bus! And even if she was Scott's sister, I am sure she is a lovely girl and not a single bit like him. I think she is quite special. don't you?"

Grace grinned and frowned down at her mother. "She seems very nice, Mama," she said. "I don't know about special. I think you've got a bit of a crush on our famous singer."

40

Margaret shrugged and giggled and twirled back to her preparation counter. "Maybe I have." She hummed a few bars of one of Jody's songs. "Maybe little crushes are what make the world go 'round."

"Mama! Jody is —" Grace stopped and felt herself blushing.

Margaret looked at her sharply. "Jody is what?" Her lighthearted expression had gone like the sun behind a sudden cloud and she looked as stern as Grace had ever known her. "What do you think Jody is, Grace?"

"Mama, this is silly . . ." Grace faltered. But her mother's eyes demanded an answer. It was a look Grace knew of old and it only came out when she had been particularly naughty. "Have you read the papers today?" She hedged.

Margaret nodded. "I've had a look at all of them," she said in a voice that still had the power to curdle Grace's stomach.

"Well, you know what I mean, then," Grace said and in her own ears her words sounded mealy-mouthed and shameful. She squared her shoulders and raised her chin. "She's a lesbian," she said and the words seemed to hang in the air between them.

Margaret regarded her daughter with unreadable eyes for longer than Grace found comfortable. Finally she asked, "Do you find that a problem, Grace?"

Grace shook her head and held out her hands, helplessly. "No, Mama, of course not."

"Then why mention it, if it isn't a problem?"

"Mama," Grace almost wailed, "you're not being fair. I just meant —" She stopped. What did she just mean? Why had she felt it necessary to bring up the subject? Maybe it *was* a problem for her. Maybe that was the problem: not that her mother was prejudiced, but that she — Grace — was. "I'm sorry, Mama," she said eventually. "I think I assumed you would have some difficulty, some prejudice, and the truth is, it is probably me who finds it difficult." She looked her mother squarely in the eye. "I apologize."

"It is Jody you should apologize to," said Margaret, her voice still stern. "I am surprised at you, Grace. Perhaps you have forgotten the stories about how your father and grandfather were discriminated against in the old days. You are too young to have been called a wog when it was a bad insult; and laughed at because of us and our funny language and strange food. But you should not forget — nobody should ever forget."

"I have not forgotten, Ma," Grace retorted angrily. "Although sometimes I think it is about time we did. All that's past now, it's a different time."

Margaret's sharp intake of breath only accentuated the color of shock and indignation that stained her olive skin. "Oh, Grace, Grace. How can you say that? Forgetting makes wars and concentration camps. Remember your friend Jilly Rubenstein? Well, her grandmother went to a concentration camp wearing a yellow star. People like Jody would have been there too."

For some minutes the silence was punctuated only by the furious rhythm of Margaret's knife, chop-chop-chopping.

Then she said, in a voice still tight with distress, "I want you to think about why you find it difficult, as you put it, my darling. What do you mean?"

Grace shook her aching head miserably. "Nothing, Mama," she whispered. "I don't know. It was stupid and thoughtless of me. Perhaps I paid too much attention to the papers, perhaps it's the way the men carry on sometimes — it rubbed off on me. Perhaps I shouldn't make excuses. I should think before I speak."

Margaret said nothing and for a while the two women worked on. Then, as the hush slowly returned to a companionable silence, there was a jaunty rap on the kitchen door. In fright, Margaret and Grace swung around simultaneously to see Jody, dressed in a faded pink T-shirt and denim cutoffs, her hair slicked back and darkly damp, her feet bare and her mouth a round *O* of surprise at the effect of her entrance.

All three regarded one another for a minute, then Margaret laughed. "And you are a dreadful young woman," she admonished Jody. "Appearing like a terrorist and frightening people to death."

"I'm truly sorry, ma'am," said Jody, looking puzzled but contrite and managing to make the expression comically spaniel-like. "Whatever I may have done, I am truly sorry."

Margaret laughed. "And I suppose you get yourself out of lots of trouble with that look," she said, her voice warm with approval.

Jody grinned. "I think my mom would agree with you, ma'am. If I'd thought about it I would have whistled before I came in like the last of the Mohicans. But I can't find my sneakers and to tell the truth, I'm enjoying your red dirt." She held up one rust-colored foot and wiggled her toes as evidence. "And I was hoping to persuade you to let me give you a hand with dinner, or something." Her eyes were round and hopeful, like those of a small girl. "I would have gone for a walk if I didn't think it would end up with me having to be rescued by the Flying Doctor or Crocodile Dundee," she explained. "So I figured I could do something useful instead." She smiled so appealingly that, after instantly suspicious thoughts that she and her mother were being sent up, even Grace was convinced that this strange American singing star was probably sincere. Margaret seemed to take even less persuasion. She held her arms wide in welcome and that was that, Jody Johnson was a kitchen hand.

After being given a crushing hug, a spare pair of white leather and wooden-soled kitchen clogs and a firm chiding from Margaret on the dangers of bare feet in kitchens, Jody's lesson in gnocchi-making proceeded apace and stretched on into the early evening. To Grace's astonishment — and reluctantly and privately admitted chagrin — she also became privy to Margaret's meatball recipe and was allowed a free hand with a fresh tureen of tomato and basil sauce for pasta. All the while, Grace went about her own chores, miserably chastened by the revelation of her own stereotypical views and the realization that there was a level of ignorance in her of which she had been utterly unaware.

But Margaret and Jody seemed heedless of her gloom and it was only when her mother asked her to take Jody to Iris's herb and vegetable garden to pick fresh leaves and lemons for the night's salads, that she had any sense that either had even been much aware of her presence. Nevertheless, as they made their way across the yard toward the brush-fenced kitchen garden, Grace felt her spirits lifting as she drank in the bronze-pink sky and sounds of birdlife preparing for nightfall. Beside her, Jody clunked along in the clogs, pretending to tap dance to a tune whistled under her breath. She carried a small basket on her arm and twirled a pair of kitchen scissors from one finger. It seemed, Grace thought, that they had known each other for years.

Unlatching the rabbit-proof gate to the garden, Grace asked Jody, "Do you know which ones to pick?"

"Your mama wants oregano, pizza thyme, tarragon, rosemary, marjoram and mint. I may have a little difficulty with the thyme and tarragon, everything else should be a breeze. But," she added quickly, "I would appreciate your help."

Clearly, she did not want Grace to go, but Grace was not about to. They moved through the neat rows of young plants and Jody marveled at the abundance, spotting lettuces of at least six varieties as well as seedlings that would become onions, garlic, tomatoes, eggplant and pumpkin vines. There was a lemon tree in one corner, a lime tree in another, and a rambling rose covered the west-facing fence with a profusion of fragrant white flowers.

"How does this all grow here?" she asked in wonder. "This is practically desert, isn't it?"

"My grandmother has been cultivating this patch for forty years," said Grace. "What she doesn't know about organic fertilizer isn't worth knowing, and there's a drip irrigation system that my father ran in from the creek. Before that, my grandfather used to bring it up in forty-gallon drums on the back of the truck, then he installed a pump and about five years ago Papa worked out a solar pump. It only fails for about six weeks of the year if the creek dries up and then we switch to rainwater tanks. It makes the roadhouse just about self-sufficient in important things — tasty things."

"It's wonderful. This is an amazing place. I can't believe it. No wonder you came back here."

"Ah," said Grace and her grin was more than halfway to a grimace. "Funny thing is, I haven't really lived here for years. First there was boarding school, then university; then I got married." She sniffed at a lemon and twisted the fruit free of its stalk and dropped it into Jody's basket.

Jody waited a minute. Then: "Is that it?" she asked, kneeling and snipping at the oregano bed. "Do I get to know more or is it still private?"

Grace perched on an upturned water drum and watched Jody for a moment before continuing. "No, it's not particularly private, I don't think. It just isn't terribly interesting. My father had a heart bypass operation and they needed help. My marriage went wrong and luckily I had somewhere to run to where I could be useful."

"It must have gone very wrong for you to run away," Jody said softly. She stood up and regarded Grace with serious eyes. "You don't strike me as being a person to run home to mama at the first fight . . ."

Grace smiled and shrugged. "It went very, very wrong," she conceded. "More wrong than I could have believed possible. I didn't so much run away as run for my life. You can take out restraining orders but the police aren't usually very interested until you are actually dead or spectacularly badly shot up." She twisted another lemon off its stalk with a decisive snap.

"Oh, jeez," Jody whispered. "I'm so sorry. I didn't

mean to be flippant." Impulsively she put out her hand and Grace took it, enjoying the reassuring pressure and the warmth of feeling that glowed in Jody's face. "Looks like we almost got off to a bad start," she said sheepishly. "Maybe we can begin again and be friends? You told me your secret, now I'll tell you mine — how about it?"

Grace nodded and smiled, but then Margaret's voice cut through the still evening. Oregano was urgently wanted.

Jody grinned and snapped her fingers. "Rats," she said mischievously, "I guess you'll just have to take a rain check."

By the end of the evening on the day the Jody Johnson Band descended on Barralong Creek, Grace knew herself to be uncommonly exhausted. It was a mixture of the weariness that was inevitable after close to eighteen hours of physical work and the drained-out emotions of a see-sawing day of unexpected highs and equally surprising lows. Reluctant though she was to leave the gathering that lingered in the restaurant, she was also aware that another long day was only six hours away.

While Jody effortlessly plucked out on the top strings of her guitar the mandolin part to an Italian folk song that Iris and Tony were teaching the others, Grace slipped away from the group and out into the crisp spring night. She listened to the harmonies and laughter for a few minutes then walked around the back of the building toward her own cabin. Like Jody's, it was set apart from the rest and in front of it was a small rustic bench. Grace sat down and stretched back to take in the stars and the peaceful night. She breathed deeply and gradually felt the aches and pinched muscles of her back and shoulders begin to loosen and relax. After a while she eased off her shoes, wiggled her toes and sighed a sigh of deepest relief.

"I could kiss 'em for you, that'd make 'em feel good," said Red Douglas's unmistakable voice out of the dark. Grace leapt to her feet as he approached her, ambling from the shadows of one of the big old pepper trees that sheltered different parts of the yard. His thumbs were thrust into the belt loops of his jeans so that his long fingers curled protectively and ostentatiously around the prominent bulge of his crotch.

"You startled me," Grace said, not bothering to disguise the irritation in her voice.

"That's a shame," Red said softly. He stopped in front of her and swayed gently back and forth. "I've been waiting for you. Thought we could have a little drink, get to know each other a bit better — have a few laughs." He held out a whiskey bottle.

Grace shook her head and took a step backwards, alarm bells clanging in her mind. "I'm very tired, Red," she said in what she knew was her placating voice — the one she had used so often in talking to Scott. "It's been a long day."

Red grinned and lifted the bottle in a cavalier salute. "And it's gonna be a long night," he observed. Grace put the bench between them and stepped back again until she felt the front step of her cabin against her bare heel. "You're a nice fella, Red," she said with more conviction than she felt, "but you're not my type, if you see what I mean."

Red snorted and the grin on his face was not pleasant. "Oh yeah?" His voice was not much above a whisper, but it cut Grace to shivers. "And who would your type be, truckstop princess? I hope you're not about to make a fool of yourself over the boss lady. I saw the way you were looking at her tonight." He sniggered as he saw Grace flinch. "Oh yeah, don't think I didn't notice. So, let me tell you something, girl." He took a stumbling step forward and his shins banged into the bench; he was cursing under his breath as he straightened up.

Grace reached behind her for the door handle but was reluctant to open it, knowing how easy it would be to get herself trapped inside the cabin. She calculated her chances of getting past him and back to the kitchen door and knew they were not good either. It seemed a better option to try to brazen it out. "You're being ridiculous, Red," she said sharply. "Why don't we have coffee in the morning."

"Ridiculous, huh?" He took a pull from the bottle. "If we're talking ridiculous let me tell you a few truths about Miz Jody Johnson. You're making eyes at the wrong one if you think you can have yourself a tumble with her. She doesn't go to bed with anyone but that ol' guitar of hers, so I can tell you, girl, there ain't no use hoping she'll pluck your strings. If you want a good time you come see Uncle Red."

"Red, you couldn't show a barn door a good time right now." Jody's voice cut sharply through the night as she strode across the yard from the main building. "Now, why don't you quit making a fool of yourself and get back to your cabin." She placed herself between Red and Grace and stood, arms folded, waiting.

Red swayed back and forth, his hand gripping the bottle as if he would like to use it as a club. But instead he took an unsteady step backwards. "Goddammit to hell Jody, why can't you mind your own goddamn business." His voice was instantly reduced to a whiny whisper.

"It is my business if you bring my name into disrepute," Jody said sharply. "And while you're a member of this band, let me remind you that you travel under my name. Now get out of here." For the longest moment neither moved. "You've got a long day tomorrow, Red, and I'm relying on you."

For another half-minute Red's hand worked the neck of the bottle, then he sighed explosively and wheeled away, "Goddamn you, Jody," he muttered over his shoulder. "You ain't queer, you're just really weird." And with that unintentionally droll remark spat into the night, he disappeared into the shadows.

Jody watched him until she was sure he had gone then she turned to Grace and lifted her shoulders. "What can I say?" she asked comically. "He's right, of course, I can't mind my own business and I *am* weird. But I'm sorry he hassled you. He's had the hots for you from the minute we arrived."

Grace shrugged, "It's fine — really. But I'm glad you happened to come out, I must admit."

"I didn't just happen. He followed you out and I was afraid there might be some trouble. He's harmless really, but that's not the point, is it?"

Grace shook her head, then she smiled. "Well, it's

my turn to ask you if you would like a drink with me." She gestured to her cabin. "I have some very nice white wine, chilled."

Jody's hesitation was infinitesimal, then she sighed. "That would be a perfect end to an amazing day," she said slowly. "But I think I have to take another rain check. That is, if you have rain checks out here ..." She looked up at the clear starry sky.

The sinking feeling of regret and embarrassment hit the pit of Grace's stomach even as she nodded her understanding. "That's fine," she said. "Let's make it another time." And before Jody could say or do anything else, Grace was gone. Inside, she leaned against the door and was bewildered at the sharp prick of tears that welled up. I am over-tired, she told herself. Over-tired and over-emotional and I need a shower and some sleep. She was right, and later, cool between cool sheets, she lay listening to the night sounds. She knew Jody had been entirely practical and sensible, but she still tossed and turned and wished for something indefinable and just out of reach.

CHAPTER FOUR

Grace was up at six and feeling, she decided as she stood once again under the soothing jets of hot water, like death only very slightly warmed up. As she made her way across to the kitchen, she sent a telepathic message of thanks to Jody for turning down the invitation to drink yet more wine. Her mother was busy already, making enormous breakfasts for the truckers who would soon be on the road all day.

"You look tired, my darling," Margaret commented as she flipped sausages and checked eggs.

"I feel tired, Mama," Grace admitted. "Do you want me to take over here?"

"That would be marvelous. Your father will be up later. He too looks a little the worse for wear this morning! But never mind, he had a wonderful evening. It was so good to hear him and Iris singing, don't you think?"

Grace nodded as she tied the strings of a large red and white striped apron. "It was a lovely evening."

"Did you have a nightcap with Jody?" Margaret's eyebrows had a way of looking artless that Grace recognized from way back.

She grinned and shook her head, "No, Mama." Then she added, "We decided we were too tired."

Margaret pursed her lips and nodded. "Very sensible of you," she said.

Grace closed her mouth firmly before she could tell her mother that it had been Jody's sensible idea, not her own. At the same time she could not make out the expression, nor the possible motive, that lay at the back of Margaret's apparently guileless smile. If she could think of any logical reason why, she would have sworn that her mother was encouraging her friendship with the visitor. But it made no sense and she decided to put the puzzle out of her mind in the face of a flurry of heated activity.

The morning whipped by in a blur of eggs cooked in every conceivable fashion. The pace was something that Grace enjoyed. It was absorbing but easy and the physicality of it was good too — especially for someone whose normal work consisted of hours of careful inaction while watching and photographing wild birds, followed by further hours bent over a drawing board or easel painting brilliant but anatomically accurate portraits of her feathered subjects.

Sometimes, Grace thought, cooking anything up to one hundred trucker-size breakfasts was just the antidote to the esoteric world of an ornithological artist. And sometimes, she thought again as hot fat sputtered up from a griddle full of eggs and stung her forearms, it was not. Nevertheless, it was good to know that by two o'clock she would be untying her apron strings and heading out in the old truck on a drawing expedition. And before that, she decided, she would have thought up some suitable farewell quip to Jody about rain checks.

But as she finished the sixty-fifth egg of the morning, Grace was no closer to anything that remotely qualified as a quip. Saying good-bye to somebody before there was much of a chance to know them didn't really lend itself to quips, she mused. She was still trying to come up with something suitably light-hearted when her father came bustling into the kitchen.

"Disaster, *cara,* disaster," he boomed dramatically.

"How come, Papa?" Grace asked, keeping a watchful eye on a tray of bacon.

"Those fools in Adelaide have not got the right spare parts. The bus is going nowhere today." He spiked two orders on the shelf in front of her. "This is for Mr. Ed, *cara,* give him extra bacon, okay? And this is for those backpackers. I think they could do with two eggs each — they don't seem to have much money and they are very thin."

He was gone before Grace could make her traditional comment about how come he didn't just give their customers the profits and save her the bother of cooking? But his bustling exit meant that she had a private moment to feel the tiny explosion of elation that lit a fireworks display within her. It reminded her, suddenly, of how she had felt the first time her best friend at school, Claris Carver, had invited her home for the half-term break. It had been one of those holidays that color all others and make them magical in memory. She and Claris had spent the week running wild on the Carvers' property and, at nine years old, had kissed each other with chaste passion and declared their undying love for each other the night before they were shipped back to school. Claris had been the first of her school friends to die — at eighteen in a car accident — but for Grace they would always be nine years old and plotting their escape to London, New York, Paris or even — they had once decided in a rare moment of pragmatism — Sydney.

"Cara! The bacon! You are burning the bacon!" Tony was back in the kitchen with another order; and, indeed, several ends of bacon were gently on fire.

Grace pulled the tray from beneath the element and blew out the flames. "Sorry Papa, miles away." She shook herself and determined to concentrate properly. The dizzy feeling as she had bent to the bacon also reminded her to eat something and she fished the slightly charred bits from the tray and quickly sliced a fresh tomato to make herself a sandwich.

By three o'clock she had finished her stint in the kitchen, showered and changed and was preparing to head off on an expedition. She had a commission for a series of paintings of a rare local bird — a sub-species of the yellow, green and black Port Lincoln parrot — and there was a billabong not far from Barralong where she had discovered a colony of the spectacular little birds. As she was packing her gear into the old truck Jody came out of her cabin and sauntered over. It was the first time she had been sighted all day, and she looked more than a little the worse for wear.

"Did you sleep well?" Grace asked innocently and was not surprised by the shake of the tousled blonde head that was her only answer. "Have you eaten?"

Again Jody shook her head, but this time she also managed a croaky, "No." She ran her fingers through her hair and shook herself like a dog. "No, I haven't, but I'm not hungry," she said, yawning and stretching. "Where are you off to, anyway? Is it anywhere I can go too?"

"I've got to do some work for a project," Grace said, suddenly protective of her work and her beloved billabong. "I'm sure you'd be bored."

Jody sighed and looked absurdly downcast. "I won't get in the way," she said. "Please say yes."

Grace hesitated, weighing up the pleasant idea of company against the probable tension of feeling responsible for somebody like Jody who would find it all dreary and pointless after twenty minutes. Then Margaret came out of the kitchen carrying a covered basket and beamed at her guest.

"Are you going with Grace, Jody?" she asked looking from one to the other expectantly.

Jody shrugged. "I don't know whether I'm

allowed," she said half-seriously, half-amused. "I'll probably be a terrible nuisance."

"Nonsense. Take her," Margaret said to Grace in tones that brooked no dispute. "She has been sitting in that room too long already. She needs some fresh air. And you," she said to Jody, "will be surprised at how beautiful our part of the country is. Not just this dusty old highway. Believe me." She held out the basket. "And there are enough emergency supplies here for two." Jody grinned and took the basket.

Grace was vaguely irritated. She enjoyed her time alone away from the bustle of the truckstop and, more than that, she did not want to have to look after Jody — and maybe get teased too. But both Margaret and Jody were smiling at her in a way that made refusal an out-of-the-question piece of churlishness. She took the basket from Jody as graciously as she could and said only, "Hop in, then. Let's get going." And Jody waved jauntily to Margaret as they drove off.

Grace's goal was another creek lined with massively elegant river red gums that meandered across the flats of an abandoned cattle property about fifteen miles from Barralong. As she drove, Grace explained the location. "I found it a couple of months ago after I'd been watching which way the parrots seemed to go. It's where they like to gather toward late afternoon and early evening; they go to feed and take a drink. It's a beautiful spot — and since the old fella who ran the place went into a nursing home a couple of years ago, it's unknown to most people because it's just been let go wild."

"How long have you painted birds?" Jody asked as she craned her neck to catch every new sight and sound.

"Since I was a kid," Grace replied, "but now I do it better."

"You must be pretty good if you get commissioned."

Grace shrugged. "Not many people do this kind of work."

"I don't suppose many can," Jody shot back. "Not to your standard anyway."

"How do you know about my work?"

Jody's grin widened. "Well, after I left you with all good intentions to get a good night's rest, I couldn't sleep a wink — that's why I look so dismal — so I went for a walk, looking for something to drink and some company and lo and behold, I found your mother. She showed me your portfolio."

A groan escaped Grace's throat but was cut short as she maneuvered the heavy truck around a burned-out tree stump and onto a dirt track. They bounced along it in low gear until it joined another trail that widened into a slightly better, recently graded surface. Then Grace asked, "What else did she show you, or tell you?"

"Oh, she just politely answered a lot of questions put to her by a curious and insomniac guest. Nothing much." Jody frowned at Grace's tortured expression. "Really, nothing that you probably wouldn't tell me if I asked you."

Grace had a pretty good idea how much Jody might have wheedled out of her mother. But in truth, she didn't mind too much. Jody was trying to relax in her seat and hang on at the same time as the truck's springs rhythmically squealed and complained at the rutted surface of the track.

"This is the old access road. It's used as a fire trail too," Grace said, as she cranked the truck into second gear. "There's a locked barrier at the highway. Nobody comes down here much anymore and nobody is doing much by way of maintenance either." She stopped talking to wrestle with the steering wheel as the rear tires slid and skittered in deep red sand. Jody hung on and braced her legs as she watched Grace's expert handling of the hefty vehicle. Grace caught her gaze out of the corner of her eye and laughed. "You okay?" she yelled above the roar of the engine.

"Never been better," Jody yelled back.

Grace parked the truck in the shade of a stand of lacy jade green gum trees and switched off the engine. The silence was deafening and profound. All around them the bush undulated in waves of pale and paler greens and blues to the horizon, like an inland ocean of vegetation. For a moment there was no sound at all, then the birds, which had fallen silent at their noisy approach, decided all was well again and went back to their busy fluting and whistling. Down a rough leaf-strewn slope toward the creek a mob of magpies took up their caroling conversation where they'd broken off. A breeze intermittently stirred the high treetops, and in every way it was as if Grace and Jody were the only human beings alive.

Jody was clearly enchanted by the scene and without pause wandered off through the trees in pursuit of the magpies' song. Grace breathed a sigh of relief and hoisted her backpack of equipment onto one shoulder, gripped Margaret's basket in her free hand and picked her way down toward the creek bank and her favorite spot. Checking once again that Jody looked happy puttering about farther down the creek, Grace took out her binoculars, a sketch pad and pencil and, after five minutes' intent observation of a group of birds, began a series of quick sketches of the parrots as they flirted about the treetops and creek banks. Soon she had forgotten her guest and was entirely absorbed in transferring the fleeting glimpses of colors and movements onto paper.

After a while Grace saw Jody tiptoe quietly across the clearing, carefully avoiding fallen branches, snappy twigs and the deeper leaf litter. She flopped down on the rug beside her. "Do you mind if I watch?" she asked in a low voice.

Without looking up Grace shook her head. "No, not at all. I'm sorry I can't stop, I just want to get this down." She continued, with sure strokes of the brush on glistening wet paper, to translate the upward sweep of a parrot's wing as it landed on a branch. "Are you bored?"

"Not at all," Jody said firmly. "I just wish I had brought my notebook. The ideas are falling over each other." She stretched out on the rug and peered through her laced fingers at the leaf canopy above them. "This is a beautiful place."

"Would you like some drawing paper? There are plenty of spare pencils in the box too."

Jody sat up. "I'd love some paper. It doesn't matter what it is — don't give me your beautiful drawing paper."

"Beautiful drawing paper is all I have and you're

welcome to it." Grace ripped several sheets from the bottom of the block and handed them over. Within minutes both had retreated into their own private worlds with only the sound of pencils on paper sighing into the other sounds of the afternoon.

At least an hour later, as the light faded and began to turn the afternoon to rose and gold, Grace suddenly realized how the time had flown. Jody was nowhere in sight and there were no tell-tale snapping of twigs or bird alarm calls to indicate that she was close by. Grace packed away her drawing materials and wondered, guiltily, where Jody had gone and whether she was bored stiff. She set off back toward the high point where the truck was parked — and came upon Jody sprawled full length in the hammock-like white-bark-smooth fork of a fallen gum tree, watching Grace's progress from slitted eyes beneath the brim of her hat. Without knowing why, Grace felt shy and simultaneously annoyed with herself for being self-conscious. "I'm sorry I took so long," she said abruptly. "You should have said something."

Jody grinned at her and sat up. "Nothing to say. I finished what I was doing. You hadn't. And I was the one who busted in on your afternoon. Anyway, it's beautiful up here. Come sit down and enjoy the view."

Grace hesitated but then felt even sillier as the grin on Jody's face broadened and she realized, with painful embarrassment, that the American knew exactly the thought that had flitted through her mind. "I said come and enjoy the view," Jody said lightly. "I don't bite. Or make passes."

"I didn't —" Grace stopped when she felt herself blushing. "Are you always so cocky and obnoxious?" she asked sharply. "Is that what being a famous star does for you?"

The expression on Jody's face made her instantly wish she could have bitten out her tongue. "I'm sorry," she said quietly, sitting on the log beside Jody. "I'm really sorry." Impulsively she touched Jody's hand and squeezed it uncertainly. For a moment Jody's hand remained inert, then she nodded and her fingers returned the gentle pressure in a way that Grace found friendly and reassuring.

"I'm sorry too," Jody said softly. "I didn't mean to be cocky, and I certainly didn't mean to be obnoxious."

"You're not, you're not," Grace said anxiously. "I don't know why I said that. You've been perfectly nice and I like you, but . . ." She shrugged helplessly, bewildered by her own behavior.

"But you've had enough of bullies who want to play the big star and have you jump to and salute. Is that about right?"

Grace stared hard at her, unable to believe she had heard correctly. "What do you mean?" she whispered. "How do you . . ."

Jody's green-blue eyes were twinkling and a gentle smile curled the edges of her mouth. "Like I said before, your mother is a lovely woman," she said wryly. "When a body can't sleep it's real good to find a cup of coffee and someone who will tell you stories and answer all those questions." She smiled. It was a hopeful and mischievous expression.

Grace nodded slowly. "My mother should be shot," she said firmly, but she too smiled.

For a while they sat watching the western sky turning an ever deeper shade of indigo as puffs of cloud picked up splashes of deep pink. Streaks of red, pink and gold flared high above them as the molten gold ball of the sun colored the landscape and the birds settled for the night.

"We could be the only people in the world," Jody said.

Grace shivered — with pleasure, not chill. "I know. At times like this I realize I'm very lucky to be able to come here. No matter how bad you might be feeling, it will always make you feel better."

"And when you're already feeling good, it makes you feel . . ." Jody gestured toward the sun, touched her hand to her heart and frowned for a moment, as if trying to form the thought properly. She looked at Grace closely, her eyes darker than before and seeming to see right into Grace's mind. "When you're feeling good," she said slowly, "and you see that setting sun, it's like . . . it's like a heart on fire."

Grace smiled and nodded, unable to speak. She knew exactly what Jody meant because, in that moment, her heart *was* on fire — with the loveliness of the evening and with the warmth and tenderness of the woman in whose hand her own was still loosely clasped. Somewhere she could hear an alarm bell ringing, but it was a feeble sound and the peace and beauty of the moment in which they were caught was overwhelming; and Grace knew only that she wanted to be in it, without any thought for the past or future.

CHAPTER FIVE

Back at the truckstop the members of the band were getting ready to have a party. There was a fax in Ed's top pocket confirming that a mechanic would be arriving from Adelaide in the morning and, once Ol' Tammy was fixed, they'd be on the road again. "Much as they enjoy your cooking, they want to move on," an apologetic Ed told Margaret. "You know what boys are like. There are girlfriends who're meeting up with us at the rodeo."

But Red Douglas was the exception. He had put two and two together when he found, as he restlessly prowled the perimeter, that both Jody and Grace were missing from the compound.

"Where are the love birds?" he asked Margaret sardonically when he went into the restaurant for a cold drink. A frown creased her forehead. She had not fallen for the handsome guitarist's obvious charm and she was not pleased by his assumption — especially since it was accompanied by a grin she could only think of as lewd.

"What do you mean?" she asked him in an unusually glacial tone.

Red's grin remained wide and mean. "Princess Grace and my boss lady, Miz Jody Johnson," he said, seeming to snip off each word between his gleaming white, wolf's teeth.

"Grace has to work and Jody went along for the ride," Margaret said between tight and reluctant lips.

"Work, huh?" Red laughed raucously. "She'll have to work hard on that one," and there was a sneer in his voice. "Jody's not a push-over, y'know, never mind what the papers say."

Before Margaret could make the angry retort that was on the tip of her tongue a voice behind her cut in. "You should know about being a push-over, my friend." Jody's voice was hard and her expression caused Red to take a step back from the counter, even though Jody was behind it.

"Hey, just kidding, girl. Just kidding," he said, swallowing hard. He saw Grace standing behind Jody and the expression on her face was unreadable. He grinned hopefully. "Hey, Gracey, babe," he said, half-laughing but nervous. "Tell her not to take it so seriously, okay? We're on the road. I'm teasing. Having fun. It don't mean nothing."

Grace's face was like stone. "You're on the road," she agreed. "It means nothing, I know that."

Jody turned and looked at her helplessly, but with Red's mocking gaze and Margaret's anxious eyes skewering her, she felt unable to speak.

Grace looked at her skeptically, her head cocked on one side. "Wouldn't you agree, Jody?"

For a moment all Jody could hear was the way Grace's voice sounded as she said her name. She knew she was behaving like a schoolgirl and she felt powerless to respond adequately. She shook her head and looked to Margaret for assistance. Margaret took Jody's arm and broke the tension.

"Come, Jody. Before we think about dinner, come and have some very delicious cheese and a glass of good red wine with me in the kitchen." Her voice was reassuring. "Grace, I know it's your night off but would you mind helping out? We're going to be busy." She patted Jody on the hand. "You don't know this but the Jody Johnson Band is doing an extra and unscheduled charity concert tonight."

The country night at Davanzo's instantly became part of the folklore of the region. Somehow, the word had spread around through the bush telegraph, and battered farm trucks and utes piled in from miles around. There were also upwards of thirty huge long-haul trucks in the car park. Grace hardly had time to take any of it in, she was so busy dishing up steaming plates of Davanzo specialties to what seemed to be an endless stream of hungry people. Eventually the demand for food dried up and Grace was able to escape the kitchen and pour herself a glass of wine.

The band had set themselves up in a corner of the restaurant and, Jody explained to the delighted audience through the sole microphone, were going to play "unplugged. So let's pretend we're on MTV, okay?" She took up her gleaming deep-bodied guitar, then checked her tuning against Levine's fiddle and Red's mandolin. Darren Juneau hauled his double bass to the standing position and ran through a series of chords and notes, Ben's brushes beat out an experimental flourish on a single snare drum and hi-hat cymbal, then Jody turned to the others, snapped her fingers and called "A-one-two-three-four," and they were away. And as everyone present quickly realized, although the band was without its customary sound and light rig, the roadhouse audience were not going to be short-changed in the slightest.

The five ran through their full concert program and then, when the stamping, cheering and clapping showed no sign of abating, they improvised through a set of classic country hits that were requested and sung along with by their ecstatic listeners. More than two hours later Jody went down on one knee before a laughing Margaret and called, "And this one is especially for the finest cook in Australia!" Red bent over the mandolin and spun the opening notes of Patsy Cline's last hit as Jody began to sing, "I — fall — to pieces . . ." before she was almost drowned out by howls of appreciation and merriment.

Watching her mother's entranced face and catching the similarly rapt expressions in the eyes of the roomful of ordinary, unglamorous, unsophisticated country people, Grace found herself fully comprehending the power and depth of Jody's talent. It was as if her soaring voice and the warmth of its expression reached out around the room and touched everyone in it, capturing them within an intangible but inescapable web of communal good feelings.

She *is* a star, Grace thought. Now I understand what that means.

Then, to her surprise, as the tumultuous applause eventually began to subside, Jody held up her hand and called for quiet. "Okay, everyone," she yelled. "Have you been having a good time tonight?" The audience stomped and banged tables in thunderous assent. "Okay, that's good, so now it's time to pay."

Grace caught her mother's eye and raised her eyebrows, but Margaret simply frowned and lifted one finger to her lips.

"You all know Jenny." Jody pointed to where the waitress was standing by the counter looking both exhausted and puzzled. "Jenny is part of Davanzo's and Davanzo's is part of this crazy old world of truckin' and travelin' and we'd all be hungrier and unhappier if we couldn't come here once in a while. Ain't that right?"

There was another roar of agreement.

"But —" Again she held up her hand for quiet. "But I wonder if you know what Jenny's going through right now?"

Jenny looked toward Margaret, who shrugged and smiled.

"Jenny has a little girl and some of you've probably seen her here in the restaurant. And some of you might be wondering why you haven't seen her lately. Well, the answer is, she's in the hospital down in Adelaide and she needs to see a specialist and have some weird treatment before she can come home. That treatment is awfully expensive, and there's the catch. If Jenny pays for the treatment she can't afford to go and be with her little girl. And that kid needs her mom if she's gonna get through this and come home."

"Pass the hat!" a stentorian voice in the crowd yelled. "Pass the hat!"

"So," Jody said, grinning, "we're gonna pass the hat for Jenny and her little girl and I'm gonna start it rolling now." She took off her hat and dropped a $50 bill into it. There were gasps and squeals across the room and then the band powered into a rollicking old-style barn dance tune as the hat began to make the journey around the room.

Late that night when the last rowdy farm truck had tooted and disappeared into the night and the last truckie had taken to his bunk, Grace left her mother, Jenny and Jody deep in conversation and money-counting and took a glass of wine out to the back step to sit in the darkness, listening to her feet complaining and her back groaning. It had been a wonderful night, she thought wearily but happily, and she had to agree with her mother, Jody was something very special indeed. When she heard footsteps behind her, she turned toward the sound, smiling, half-expecting to see her mother.

"Waiting for me, are ya?" Red grabbed her hand and pulled her up and into his arms so swiftly that the wine slopped out of her glass and down her jeans. His mouth tasted of stale beer and cigarettes and she struggled grimly to release herself, but Red was muscled and determined. "Aw, c'mon," he protested, pulling her roughly into his arms and dragging at the buttons of her shirt. "I know you like me and you won't be getting nowhere with the boss. I told you she's a queer fish."

Red's assumptions, as much as his unwelcome attention, caused Grace to continue to struggle fiercely, twisting and turning to avoid having his mouth planted wetly and odorously on hers. "Let go of me," she whispered vehemently. She was desperate not to be found in such a ridiculously unpleasant position and especially desperate not to alert her mother or Jody. A button ripped off her shirt and his fingers momentarily clutched at her breast. Furious at the sensation and at her so recent casual encouragement of him and at what he had just said, she eventually managed to win herself the leverage to lash out with all her strength and, as luck would have it, clip him on the side of his ankle. Her hard-toed boot caught the bone just as a strong, long-fingered hand slammed down on his shoulder from behind. It was Jody.

"I think Grace wants you to leave her alone," she said quietly, her fingers gripping the guitarist's shoulder like a vise. Red was gasping with pain from his hacked ankle and in furious response, he tried to take a swing at Jody who ducked away easily. "Don't be even more stupid than you already are, Red," she said wearily. "Now get out of here and go to bed. This time you really do have a long drive tomorrow."

For what seemed like an age but, Grace knew, was only about ten thumping beats of her heart, Red glowered at Jody and Jody stared right back. Their eyes were on a level but somehow Red seemed smaller. Finally he cursed viciously, almost spitting in Jody's face, then he stumbled off across the yard, swearing and limping.

Grace caught her breath and struggled to straighten her clothes and effect some kind of order on her torn shirt; embarrassment and relief swirled through her in disconcerting waves. "You always seem to be rescuing me," she said in mild exasperation. "I can usually take care of myself."

Jody chuckled. "I am sure you can. I wouldn't like to see his ankle tomorrow morning. But the silly fool deserved it. You okay?"

"Sure. He had too much to drink."

"It was a big night. One of the best. I'm really sorry."

"It's okay, honestly. I just need to soak these jeans — they're my best ones and they're covered in red wine."

"Maybe we should go throw salt all over you!" Even in the dark Grace knew that Jody's eyes were twinkling.

"Maybe we should just have a quiet glass of wine and put our feet up. I don't know about you but mine are yelling blue murder."

Jody flexed the fingers of her left hand and examined the calloused fingertips. "Yeah, well, I've never heard it put that way but I know what you mean. It was a pretty amazing night, and you and Jenny must have run twenty miles. Your place or mine?"

"I have that bottle of good dry white that I offered you before — chilled. What about you?"

"A couple of beers. I think you win."

They walked across the yard to Grace's cabin which, from the outside, was much the same as the rest, but inside was a world of difference. Here a sofa, armchair and small table and chairs clustered at the base of an L-shape divider, with a fridge beneath. This set off the sleeping area, which Grace had made even more private with an all-enveloping square-draped mosquito net. She had also added touches to the interior that made it quite different. On the blond wood-paneled walls were lengths of fabric printed in the warm earth colors and traditional designs of central Australian Aboriginal women. It gave the room the effect of being a richly colored tent, and the tumble of big squashy cushions on the floor and a quilt on the bed, all covered in similar fabric, helped fill the place with a feeling of life and comfort.

"This is lovely," Jody said, looking around. She flopped down naturally and without fuss on the cushions and Grace found herself feeling at ease in a way she would never have imagined possible. She retired to the bathroom to pull off the grape-stained jeans, dropped them in a bucket of water, wrapped a sarong around herself and tucked it expertly and neatly across her breasts. She checked the effect in the mirror — casual, but not particularly revealing — and took two deep breaths before rejoining Jody, who had opened the bottle of wine and poured two generous glasses. They were soon into conversation, ranging from chunks of life history to their ideas about the things that mattered to them. Right away Grace had forgotten her aching legs — comfortably stretched the length of the sofa — and time slipped by as their acquaintance traveled a distance that could otherwise have taken years — or never. She listened to Jody's loving descriptions of her childhood home on the sea's edge of the wild and harshly beautiful Oregon coast and began to understand, from the way she spoke, where the everyday easy poetry of her song lyrics came from. And Jody drew out of Grace the stories of her unusual childhood as the only daughter of a family whose isolated business had unwittingly given her the gift of loving and understanding the wilderness by which she was surrounded. It was a point of mutual recognition and understanding, even though geographically and climatically so seemingly opposite.

Eventually, Jody stretched and caught sight of her watch. Her eyes widened. "Lord, have mercy," she said in mock horror. "It's four o'clock."

Grace gasped and laughed as they both got to their feet. In that instant she felt the strangest mixture of inevitability and exhilaration as Jody took her in her arms.

"I've never talked like this with anyone," she said, looking down at Grace, a puzzled, wary expression on her face.

Grace slid her hands up Jody's arms, enjoying the unexpected musculature beneath the heavily embroidered shirt sleeves. "Me neither."

For a moment they stood looking at each other, then slowly and deliberately, so that — Grace understood later — she had plenty of opportunity to stop it if she wished, Jody bent her head and kissed her. And Grace made no move to avoid it. It started in a tentative way as soft mouth met soft mouth, then as her heart began to race unbearably, Grace reached up to clasp Jody's neck and pull her in closer and harder.

Jody took her lead and swiftly the kiss grew more passionate as their mouths opened to the seeking pressure of the other. Grace lost herself in the sensation of the long, lean but yielding curved body pressing into her own, unhindered by the fine cotton sarong. Her head spun as Jody's tongue touched hers and the instant explosion of feeling triggered an uncontrollable yearning to be closer and closer and deeper inside. As Jody's hands slowly traversed the bare skin of her shoulders and the length of her back, Grace heard herself moan with an intense desire to have her touch and hold and explore her body — a body which she could feel opening up and flooding with a desperate longing of whose existence she had no prior knowledge.

But even as Grace's hunger impelled her forward, Jody suddenly drew away. "Grace," she whispered, "no, no . . ." She tried to pull away but Grace only held her more urgently and her tongue searched for Jody's with tender but absolute insistence.

"Please . . ." she murmured, her lips caressing the lines of Jody's mouth. "Please . . ."

The craving to feel Jody's body on her own was almost unbearable and the sound of her own heartbeat was thunderous but insufficient to drown out Jody's repeated, "No, no, no . . ."

Finally, with a desperate sigh, Jody broke away and her eyes were darkly troubled. "We'll be on the road in the morning," she said wretchedly. "We'll be gone. I can't do this, Grace. I just can't."

Grace stared at her in disbelief, her breath

coming in painfully short gasps, and she knew she had never been so utterly revealed nor so firmly and caringly spurned. She didn't know whether to laugh or cry as she stared up into Jody's agonized eyes. After a moment she almost did both as she shook her head and said bitterly, but with every last vestige of pride-saving humor she could muster, "After all these years I finally meet a decent human being who, of all things, turns out to be a fly-by-night country singer." She stepped back and, ignoring the crazy beat of her heart and the tears that pricked at her eyes, she smiled calmly. "You are quite something, Jody Johnson." She opened the door.

In the doorway Jody paused and looked at her with eyes so sad that Grace could not bear to hold their study. She reached up and gave Jody one small kiss on her unmoving lips and touched her face tenderly, then Jody shook her head sorrowfully and disappeared into the shadows of the silent pre-dawn gloom. Grace watched her, the picture of her straight, slim shoulders and graceful walk etching itself, she felt, indelibly into her mind just as the feel of Jody's body pressed against her own had wrought an unerasable sweet ache deep inside. Then she shut the door and leaned against it as tears coursed down her cheeks and the sour heat of frustration throbbed between her legs.

Unwillingly she found herself thinking of her ex-husband. Scott had been tall and long-legged like Jody and also had the same unusually thick, burnished gold hair. But, she recalled bitterly, his eyes had not been calm blue-flecked green, rather an impenetrable dark brown that turned to black when he was in a fury. It was difficult to imagine Jody descending into the kind of savage uncontrolled rage that had made life with Scott so difficult and, finally, so frightening. Was it simply because she was a woman? Grace wondered. But the comparisons were ridiculous, based on a fleeting similarity of looks, and even that wasn't accurate. Now she knew, from the experience of her very own tingling fingers, that the texture of Jody's hair was as silky-soft as Scott's had been wire-strong. And her strength of character was utterly unlike his shallow bravado. She remembered Jody's icy command when she had forced Red to back off her and, despite the careful rebuff, she recalled the gentle but extraordinary warmth of Jody's lips and the utterly unfamiliar and hopelessly exciting sensation of her body as she, Grace Davanzo — married woman and heterosexual right down to her lacy underwear — had pulled Jody into a closer and closer embrace.

"I've been on my own too long," she told herself aloud. But it didn't sound convincing. She sighed and scraped impatiently at the tear tracks on her face and went into the bathroom where, she hoped, a tepid shower would still the trembling in her limbs and the unaccustomed heat in her body that was still making its presence felt with unfamiliar and uncomfortable force. She stood under the jets of water, letting the sweat of the busy evening and long night drain away even as she tried to drag her thoughts from the body that had felt so breath-takingly good on hers.

"It's just my luck," she told herself, "after two years of thinking I could never feel anything again, when I do, it's caused by a woman who isn't interested enough and is leaving in approximately five hours and who I will never see again anyway. My God, what a loser!" Grace's impulse still teetered between laughing and crying and finally, she turned off the water and decided to simply dry herself and go to bed for what was left of the night.

CHAPTER SIX

By the time Grace surfaced it was after eight. She lay for a few minutes and re-ran the mental videotape of the previous night. When she came to the hours spent with Jody she couldn't stop herself using the pause button and, when it came to their kiss, the tape stopped completely and she heard herself whimper, feeling the treacherous heat flooding from her heart to her lower body. Her hands reached down to where she knew without doubt she wanted Jody to be, but the pulsating memory was unbearable and she jumped out of bed and threw herself once more under the consoling jets of the shower.

"You are going to turn into a wrinkled-up old prune if you spend much more time under the shower," she told herself. But she could think of no other comfort. As the water eased her aching body she contemplated avoiding the restaurant until after the Johnson Band bus had left, but she eventually dismissed the thought and instead dressed herself with unusual and defiant care in her second-best jeans, a body-hugging cap-sleeved black T-shirt and the high-heeled black jodhpur boots that made her legs look extra slim.

She grinned at her reflection as she finished applying licks of extra length and color to her already thick dark lashes and a subtle trace of pink to her mouth. She examined her face in the mirror. "You are hopeless, Grace Davanzo," she told herself. "No I'm not," said her other self, "I'm hopeful — maybe a bit crazy, but not totally stupid. I know this is just a fantasy and I'm enjoying it for what it is." Once again, it didn't sound convincing.

Squaring her shoulders she sauntered across the yard and into the restaurant as casually as she could. Inside there was pandemonium. Not only were there a dozen beefy truck drivers bulldozing up massive breakfasts, but the Johnson Band members were occupying a double table and there was clearly trouble in the air. She slipped behind the counter and through to the kitchen where Jenny was looking frazzled as she struggled with the components of a couple of dozen breakfast orders.

"What's going on?" Grace asked as she tied the

strings of her apron and checked the progress of the bacon griller.

"Chaos, I think," said Jenny. "The mechanic is already on his way from Adelaide but Andy thinks he's ordered the wrong part and he isn't in mobile phone range, so when he gets here, he'll have to turn around and go right back. And the bus still can't go on."

Grace's heart leapt clear of its moorings and she was grateful for the heat of the griddle, because she knew she had blushed scarlet.

For the next twenty minutes she was kept busy putting together the breakfasts Davanzo's was famous for and had time to regain her composure. At last she felt confident enough that she would not give herself away to go into the restaurant to make herself an espresso. She was aware of Red's sullen stare but, more than that, she was aware that Jody had not acknowledged her presence at all. It took only as long as the time needed to pack coffee into the container, screw it into place and flick the lever to send a steaming jet through the grounds for her heart to return to normal and even sink down into her boots. Without another glance at the band's tables Grace returned to the kitchen, wondering whether it was physically possible for a heart to become heavier than lead.

By ten the predicament was solved. Jenny excitedly bustled into the kitchen and told Grace that Andy the driver was returning to Adelaide to ensure the correct parts came back and the rest had all arranged lifts with helpful truck drivers and would be on their way within the hour. Grace's heart could sink no further and she simply said, "Isn't that good.

They must be pleased," in response to Jenny's news. She worked away doggedly in the kitchen, giving it a cleaning that it had not seen in some time.

By the time the rhythm of scrubbing had drained away a little of the melancholy that had threatened to overwhelm her, Grace was feeling quite pleased with herself and the way she had regained control of her crazily runaway emotions. Then Margaret came into the kitchen and, although she noticed the dazzling state of its surfaces and appliances, she only raised her eyebrows and made no other comment as she insisted that Grace come out to say good-bye to their guests.

Grace's heart betrayed her by plummeting a little more, but she could think of no excuse for not accompanying her mother out to where a fleet of trucks was waiting to depart with the boys of the band. Grace forced a smile as she watched their preparations to leave. They all shook hands with Margaret and Tony, hugged Jenny and exchanged back slaps and autographs with the truck drivers. Iris came out with her ancient camera and there was much jostling and shuffling as everyone was photographed with everyone else.

It took Grace some minutes to realize that Jody was nowhere to be seen. "Has Jody left already, Mama?"

Margaret looked astonished. "Good heavens, no, my darling. She hasn't told you?"

Grace shook her head. "Told me what? I haven't seen her this morning."

"She's staying behind to take care of business with the truck." Then she added in a lower voice, "Ed says it's easier for Jody because she doesn't have anybody waiting for her at the other end like the boys do. Isn't that sad?" Grace said nothing, but it didn't seem that her mother was expecting an answer because she went on, "Ed thinks she might want to use the time to do some writing. She can relax and work on her own without those dreadful boys bothering her." Margaret slipped her arm around her daughter's waist. "Perhaps you can take her on one of your trips again, my darling. You wouldn't mind that, would you? I think it's very good for her and she seemed to have such a nice time."

Whether it was embarrassment or guilt, Grace could not tell, but she was barely able to speak and could only manage a muttered, " 'Course not, Ma," as she saw Jody walking across the compound in earnest conference with Ed.

Then, after more and more poses and groupings for photographs, it was time for the trucks to be on their way and there was a final flurry of farewells. Red sidled over to Grace with a lopsided grin on his handsome face and, thinking that he was simply going to make amends and say good-bye, she let him kiss her cheek, but then he whispered in her ear, "You're gonna get a second chance, huh? Didn't manage it last night, huh?"

Furiously Grace stepped away from him, quelling an impulse to slap his face as she saw Jody watching them speculatively. Instead she smiled at Red as frostily as possible. "You wouldn't know anything, Red," she said in a low, venomous voice.

"Don't you kid yourself, princess," Red crowed. "Our Jody is a strange one and you better bet on it. I've been on the road three years with her and I ain't seen anybody get a leg over her yet."

"You *are* the limit," Grace said angrily. But she knew her rage was so quick to rise because of what had happened in the early hours of that morning. Her indignation was partially embarrassment at the way she had so wantonly thrown herself at Jody. And the tenderness with which she had been refused caused her face to flame once again and her fists to bunch convulsively with an intense desire to punch Red's lights out. Then she saw Jody's expression and her heart did an uncontrolled somersault at the wicked grin and twinkle in her eyes. Jody pursed her lips, frowned and slowly shook her head, as if she knew only too well what Grace was on the point of doing. Grace found herself smiling back in a way that would have been most revealing to an observer, and none observed more closely than Red. Grace sensed his narrowed eyes flicking from Jody to her and back again, as if computing every nuance of expression and the unconscious and effortless warmth that passed between them. He spat angrily in the red dust and flung away from the moment he could not be part of to climb aboard his ride.

CHAPTER SEVEN

By noon Davanzo's was back to normal. The
Johnson Band had gone, taking their clamor with
them. As the last truck had pulled away with klaxon
blazing Jody had disappeared to her cabin — to write,
she told Margaret.

For Grace it was a strangely disjointed and
prolonged day. For the first time in years she felt
restlessly aware of the proximity of another human
being and she knew she could do nothing about it.
More than that, she could not fully understand the
fretful and compulsive erotic desire for the company

of another woman. And neither could she comprehend what to do about it, when she thought of Jody's withdrawal and everything she had learned about her wilfully hermit-like lifestyle.

These feelings were outside her experience and she was alternately troubled and exhilarated in what slowly stretched into an uncomfortable roller-coaster of a day. The hours until late afternoon, when she could legitimately escape in the truck with her sketch book and paints, seemed destined never to pass. But finally the hands on the clock crept to four and she packed up her flask of coffee.

"Why don't you see if Jody wants to go with you?" Margaret asked her. Grace shook her head vehemently. "I'm sure she's busy or resting," she said to her mother firmly. "If she wants anything I'm sure she'll ask."

"You're right," said the already familiar melted-chocolate voice, right behind her. "And I would like to go with you. If it isn't too much of an intrusion."

Grace swung around, furious that her face was flaming and that, yet again, Jody had materialized so quickly as to completely disarm her. She tried to grin casually, but it didn't work. She suspected that her eyes and smile were sparkling almost as obviously as the beating of her heart.

"Oh hi, Jody," she said. And to her amazement her voice sounded quite normal. "You're welcome to come along, of course." She glanced at her mother who was beaming beatifically at Jody and she longed to pinch her arm and tell her to stop it!

* * * * *

85

As she drove Grace concentrated on the road as if her life depended on it. Beside her, one foot up on the dashboard, Jody appeared to be as casually at ease as Grace was not. She was even, Grace realized, whistling silently between her teeth. Perhaps, Grace suddenly thought, Jody's relaxation stemmed from an understanding that they would be — could be — good friends, that whatever had happened the night before was behind them. Perhaps the tumult in her own heart came from simple loneliness and Jody had recognized that with much more maturity and practicality than she herself had been able to muster. In a funny sort of way it was logical, she mused. After all, it made no sense at all that at the age of twenty-eight she would suddenly find herself turned on to women. She couldn't remember ever having read about *that* in the problem pages and advice columns.

A mixture of relief and disappointment began to settle around Grace's agitated heart in a way that was almost consoling. To be friends with Jody, she thought, was something she knew she would value — even though the singer would soon be out of her life and undoubtedly full-tilt back into a world where someone who worked in a truckstop on the way to nowhere would be a quaint and colorful memory. Before this new thought could plunge her into despondency, Grace impulsively took another fork of the fire trail and headed up and over a ridge.

"I thought you might like to see the original Billaluna homestead," she said. "It's one of the oldest in this part of the country."

"Great!"

Jody did not speak again as they bumped across

the rough terrain. Grace glanced at her and saw that she was intent on the surrounding countryside and, when the truck suddenly thumped into a pothole, Grace realized she had been equally intent on Jody's profile. As they lurched out of the crater Jody turned and caught her eyes and grinned disarmingly — in a clearly affectionate fashion.

The homestead stood on a bluff above a billabong and Grace stopped at the beginning of its driveway. There, an open five-bar gate hung lopsidedly from one remaining set of hinges, between fine tall gate-posts that had once been painted white. On the top bar of the gate the name *Billaluna* was still visible. The house was a long, low pale gray stone building surrounded by deep verandas; on the south-western side it was sheltered against the blast of summer sun and winter winds by four massive poplars.

"Are they Australian trees?" Jody asked, pointing at the graceful, black-green pencil-like trees.

Grace shook her head. "They would have been planted by the builder of the house. They liked to remind themselves of the old country — which was usually somewhere in Europe in those days," she said, grateful for the normalcy that Jody's response injected into the scene. In front of the house, on either side of the driveway, were formal rose beds; the massive, thorny old plants had been neglected so long that they had sent out long, straggling suckers in every direction, but here and there were clusters of exquisite old-fashioned blooms that simply added to the lonely poignancy of their setting. On the steps leading to the double doors a huge blue-black lizard lay toasting its six feet of length in the sunshine. Grace pointed to it and whispered, "Goanna."

"Is that like iguana?" Jody whispered back.

"I think so," said Grace. She put the truck into neutral and cruised down the drive. The goanna looked up and marched off, stiff-legged, disappearing with an irritated hiss into a thicket of massive camellia bushes on the eastern side of the house. She stopped the truck and they got out, each toting a rucksack of Grace's drawing materials and Margaret's insisted upon "emergency supplies."

Nothing stirred as they walked around the house, their boots scuffing the overgrown and dried grass of what had once been a lawn. At the northern extent of the house there was an empty and crumbling pond with an equally dilapidated fountain at its center. Beyond and below the bluff the old formal garden gave way to the bush and below that again, the billabong. It was a big one, its waters glittering green and gold in the afternoon sun as the massive river red gum trees surrounding it cast shadows on the forest floor. High above, the ever-present magpies caroled, and flights of parrots darted in flashes of pink and gray and green and yellow across their path as the two women picked their way down to a clearing beside the water where Grace stopped and flung out a rug.

"This is another magical place," Jody said in a voice barely above a whisper.

"I know," Grace replied, smiling. "I think this is my dreaming — I'm pretty sure I was conceived here. This is my spiritual birthplace. But my mother doesn't know I know!"

"Fantastic!" Jody whispered, chuckling as she took in the scene with even more interest. "It explains why you're so —" She stopped and they looked at each other with faces suddenly turned serious. Jody reached out a hand and then withdrew it. In a flash Grace remembered Red's words and put them together with Jody's reluctance of the previous night.

"It's okay, Jody," she said stoically. "We can just be friends."

Jody frowned. "You want to be friends?"

"If that's what you want." Grace shrugged. "That will be fine with me."

Jody laid down the rucksack she was carrying and took Grace's bag from her too; then she placed her hands on Grace's shoulders and studied her face carefully, as if searching for something. "If you want us to be just good friends, then I'll try," she said solemnly. "Because I really like you. But I have to warn you that I will find it very difficult, because the honest truth is, I want you to be much, much more."

Grace's breath caught in her throat and, as if magnetized, she stepped toward Jody. "I want us to be friends," she said in a voice she barely recognized. "Because you're probably the best friend a girl could have. But I also want more. Much more." She reached for Jody with a blind certainty that came from deep inside.

"Grace ... Grace ..." Jody whispered as Grace's hands tentatively slipped over the fine silver-blonde down of her forearms and the thin fabric of her shirt sleeves to rest on the width of her shoulders.

"I want ..." Grace stopped, unable to articulate what her body was already telling Jody. She reached up, on tiptoe, and Jody's lips and tongue traced the outline of Grace's mouth as her nipples responded instantly to the pressure of Grace's closeness. Grace felt hands explore the planes and contours of her back and throat even as she gave herself up to the ripples of sensation that began to spread out from the luscious touch of sensitively exploring fingers and allowed her own hands to echo the exploration.

"I can't stand up much longer," Jody said between short shallow breaths. "Not if you keep doing that." Gently she pulled Grace down onto the rug but Grace held back, troubled.

"I don't . . . I don't know what to do . . ." she said shyly.

Jody lay back and regarded her quizzically for a second then laughed delightedly. "Oh yes, you do," she said. "Believe me, you do." She hitched herself onto one elbow and looked into Grace's eyes and, with one finger, traced the line of her eyebrows, nose and across her lips. "Have you never done this before, sweetheart?"

Grace felt herself blushing and shook her head. "Not with a woman, no, I'm sorry."

Jody laughed again. "Sorry? What's to be sorry? I'm just a little surprised because . . ." She paused and again the quizzical look caused Grace to color up.

"Because I flung myself at you?" she demanded, chin rising defiantly.

Jody shook her head and her arm tightened around Grace, preventing her from backing off. "No, I don't mean that, you just seemed to . . . know what you want."

Grace looked into Jody's eyes and nodded helplessly. "That's true," she said. "I've never done this before, but I do know that I want you." As she spoke her thoughts aloud it was as if she were hearing the truth herself for the first time and a rush of warmth flooded through her; she found herself once again reaching for Jody with the hunger of a lifetime. "I want you so badly," she said, and her voice trembled with such pent-up longing that her words came out as a sob.

As Jody's fingers traced the shape of her head, Grace could feel the silkiness of her own cropped curls. Her mouth followed the lines of Jody's jaw, savoring the smooth skin and the fine-chiseled structure of neck and throat. Gently Jody lifted and pulled off Grace's T-shirt and sank her teeth into the fine lace that confined her breast. Grace gasped and her body arched; her fingers clutched convulsively into the silky thickness of Jody's hair. She wanted the sensation to go on and on, but Jody slipped the hooks of the bra and stroked the fabric off each breast in turn, then paused to gaze at what she had exposed.

"Oh, Jody," Grace whispered. Then her eyes opened and met Jody's; their gaze held and did not waver. Grace reached for her, gratefully, but Jody caught her fingers and kissed them; her hand slid down to the buttons of Grace's jeans and gave them a playful tug.

"Gotta get 'em off," she said softly and grinned down at Grace before enveloping her face in honey-blond hair and a probing, urgent, all-consuming kiss as she flipped open her own buttons and then turned her attention to Grace's.

As she dragged off the confining blue denim Grace thought fleetingly that she had never been so frantic before for the touch of another human being, then Jody's warm hand slid down between her legs and all thought and momentary shock vanished as she felt her own body take on its own life and rhythm and ache and open to Jody's easy and certain exploration. For a split second she knew the clutching convulsion of fear and a sharp stab of pain.

Jody gasped and withdrew, her eyes wide with bewilderment. "I'm sorry," she whispered.

But Grace shook her head frantically and clasped Jody's hand to her. "Please," she whispered, "please, I want you inside me. Please." Her breathing was ragged. Tentatively, Jody resumed her quest for her pulsating center. "Jody, please..." Grace moaned softly, then the caress of Jody's body on hers became a breathtaking contrast to the fiery trail that was blazing through her, direct from the exquisite thrust of Jody's fingers deep inside, to the waves of pleasure that Jody's tongue was raising in each tautly erect brown nipple. Even as Jody again froze at what she had unmistakably encountered, and again at Grace's undisguisable gasp of hurt, she was inexorably drawn into the even more unmistakable well of desire that Grace's body had become.

"Come for me, sweetheart," Jody whispered, her breath momentarily icing the heat of Grace's breasts. "Come for me, I want to feel you come for me." The words echoed like a mantra in Grace's ears and her body heard the tender command and responded. And she could feel a sensation that she sensed must be orgasm building like chords of music from the tips of Jody's strong musician's fingers. Deep in her the swell of it began to roll the length of her body until every extremity was tingling and trembling and she knew herself to be finally flying out of control into unknown regions of herself. Her limbs were suddenly heavy and she was helpless to reach out but she knew she was connected to life and the earth by Jody's hands playing her, holding her, letting her go, reeling her in, coaxing her to float in a universe whose colors were the green-blue of Jody's eyes. And they held her safe as her body arched and opened one last time and she cried out in fear and joy as she fell, tumbling and swirling into the world to be mysteriously reborn.

"Hush little baby, don't say a word —" From somewhere far away Grace could hear a lullaby. "Momma's gonna buy you a mocking bird —" Without moving — and she realized that she could not, as she seemed to be filled with lassitude, heavy and sweet as honey — she considered the possibilities. She knew she was lying in a gentle but firm embrace and held in place by a leg twined around her own. "And if that mocking bird don't sing . . ." Fingers curled and drew strands of her hair in time to the lazy lilt of the song that was being delivered in a voice now beloved and familiar. Consciousness flooded in like sun-up. She opened her eyes to Jody's steady gaze and the leap of her heart in response was devastating.

"You are so beautiful," she heard herself say. Jody grinned, bent her head and kissed the tip of Grace's nose.

"*You* are," she replied and went on with her lullaby and strand-by-strand arrangement of Grace's hair. "You remind me of a drawing I used to like in an old book. There were all these cherubs with petal caps of curly hair." She frowned and peered up at the treetops as if for inspiration. "Water babies," she said triumphantly. "You look like one of the water babies — you know, Charles Kingsley."

Grace snorted and laughed. " A cherub! Me! Then you must be a goddess." She looked around the green and gold cathedral-like vault of the billabong where the soaring smooth pink-gray-white branches of the red gums formed the flying buttresses. "A goddess of the forest, perhaps."

Jody blew a raspberry and laid her face on Grace's breast. Grace took her head in both hands and stroked the thick lustrous hair as her heart gave notice of the feelings that her hands strove tenderly to convey.

"Jody, Jody, what have you done to me?" she whispered to the sky.

Jody answered as her tongue wrought a fresh response from Grace's right nipple, "I made love to you, sweetheart." She propped herself back on one elbow and looked up with a mixture of deepest solemnity and wonderingly amused affection. "But you never done tole me you wuz a virgin, honey," she chirruped, in a cartoon-style, Brer Rabbit voice that was her attempt to undercut the seriousness of what she was saying.

Grace turned her head into Jody's shoulder and said nothing as a wave of ancient humiliation swept through her, momentarily blotting out the sensations that still coursed in slowly receding waves through her tingling body.

"Grace, sweetheart." Jody's arms wrapped about her in the tenderest of firm grips. "Talk to me, Grace. You have nothing to be ashamed of. Or afraid of."

But there were many false starts and long silences before Grace could begin to tell Jody, in an almost inaudible voice, the full and cruel truth of her marriage. Of a husband whose bizarre upbringing in a household of warped religious beliefs had made it impossible for him to make love to his wife in any ordinary loving way and whose own years of suffering had meant he found his greatest pleasure in her degradation.

"I have never told this to a living soul," Grace said, her face still buried in Jody's shoulder. "The only people who know are the medical staff at the hospital where I was admitted once when he . . . when he . . . when I needed stitches."

"My God," Jody whispered, stroking Grace's head with infinite care. "Why . . . didn't you go to the police? What about . . . surely what he did was against the law."

Grace shook her head. "I was twenty-two. I came from being a good Catholic girl to being a good wife. I knew nothing except that I couldn't bear for anybody to know what he did to me. Can you imagine what it would have done to my parents?"

"Grace, that's crazy! He could have killed you."

Grace sighed, settling herself even deeper into Jody's arms so that her face was buried between her breasts. "I know that now," she said. "But then . . . you have to understand that I just wanted to survive and not let anyone know what had happened to me. I'd been humiliated enough without it becoming public knowledge."

Jody frowned. "So, I don't understand — how did you get away? Where is he now?"

Grace sighed so deeply her entire body shook. "I

had a wonderful feminist lawyer. She forced a settle-
ment on him under threat of exposure. She managed
to convince him that it would hurt him more than it
would hurt me."

Jody shook her head in a mix of sorrow and
stunned disbelief. "My God. You poor baby." She
kissed the top of Grace's head and tightened her
hold. "So where is he now?"

Grace's voice, when she replied, sounded almost
disembodied, even to her own ears, so cold was its
tone, but her body trembled. "He's dead," she said.
"He was arrested after trying with a prostitute what
he used to do to me. Luckily, she wasn't such a
coward about turning him in. He committed suicide
when he couldn't buy his way out."

Jody rocked her and said nothing. High above
them, the other inhabitants of the peaceful afternoon
went about their chirping, cheerful business. The
sounds were more comforting than any words and
gradually, as time passed, Grace's shuddering subsided and she snuggled herself even closer into Jody's
embrace.

"It's funny," she said, and her voice had returned
to its normal warm timbre. "I didn't think I would
ever be able to tell anyone about that." She looked
up at Jody, holding her eyes in a clear and direct
gaze. "And now that I have, I feel better than I have
in years. It's as if it has suddenly been blown away.
It's gone."

Jody kissed the tip of her nose. "I think that's
called catharsis," she said and grinned. "Now we have
to deal with my trauma."

Grace frowned. "What's that?" she asked, full of
concern.

"Your being a virgin and all. I think I'm in shock. I need help here." Her eyes widened outrageously and she let out a huge and tremulous sigh. For a moment there was silence as Grace struggled to make the final one-way transition from past shame to present laughter, then all hell broke loose as she pulled herself free of Jody's grip and began flailing at her with the nearest weapon to hand, which happened to be a bread roll from the emergency supply basket.

"You pig!" Grace howled with mortification and laughter. "You pig! And I bet you're going to tell all the boys and you won't respect me in the morning!" She gave Jody an almighty push and Jody fell back, laughing.

"Ooo-wee! And yo daddy'll come after me with a shotgun fo' sure and I'll have to do the right thang by you. O mercy me!" Jody began to hum "The Wedding March," until Grace's pummeling became too much, then she grabbed Grace's wrists and held on hard. "Kiss me, honey," she breathed melodramatically. "What you got to lose? You is a ruined woman now!"

Even when Grace joined in as Jody gurgled with laughter and lay, eyes closed, enjoying her own joke, she became more and more aware of the gold-bronze body beside her. For the first time in her life she greedily drank in the familiar but unknown beauty of a female body. From the perfectly sculpted planes of Jody's strong face with its wide mouth and stubborn chin, her eyes were drawn on down to the geometry of collar bones and broad shoulders that were set in the well-developed symmetry of a champion swimmer. The skin of her breasts was paler, blue-veined and inviting in a way that Grace instantly understood in an almost narcissistic flash of memory; the breasts echoed the softly rounded curve of belly from which Grace's gaze was led by a drift of golden down to the tawny triangle of pubic hair that separated the muscular length of her thighs. On one ankle was a smudgy blue tattoo of a tiny lizard, on one knee a faded but fierce scar.

It was a body to worship, Grace thought, as she bent her head and took one of Jody's chocolate-dark nipples in her mouth. It seemed the most natural thing in the world to do and it began a quest in new territory that would mean, she knew in a flash of profound certainty, that she could never go back. Never could she be simply a divorced woman who would one day meet Mr. Right and live happily ever after. What that also meant for the future, she blocked out of her mind as her tongue rippled the surface of a flawless aureole and Grace heard Jody's sigh and sensed her laughing body become acquiescent.

She moved instinctively but tentatively, wanting to feel the contours and textures of Jody's flesh with her own. After a moment's hesitation she straddled Jody and leaned forward so that her own small firm breasts met Jody's. The sensation of nipple caressing nipple was heightened by the corresponding softness of tongue on tongue and Grace heard herself moaning with the astonishing pleasure of it. Her fingers fondled the lusciousness of Jody's flesh in repeated and unhurried movements that seemed to have direct connection with the nerve endings in every sensitive part of her body.

Then, with a half-sigh, half-moan, Jody reached

up and held her firmly by the hips so that as she began to move, Grace was opened to Jody's upward thrust. It was a sensation as light as a feather's kiss but its driving insistence built a fire within Grace's body that began to consume her, until all sensation seemed to emanate from the rhythm of Jody's fleeting touch. Again Grace could feel herself losing control as the fire raged and spread and engulfed her until finally she could burn no more and her body arched up in one, two, three, four, five spasms of purest, deepest, darkest ecstasy. As she tumbled into it she cried out into the silent afternoon, "Jody, Jody, Jody!" and her pleasured anguish was absorbed by the sunshine and Jody's welcoming arms.

With a supreme effort of determination, Grace did not slip again into the beckoning unconscious bliss. She lay panting in Jody's embrace, listening with unaccustomed joy to the heart that was thumping strongly within the breast beneath her ear. Again she whispered Jody's name, but this time the wonderment in her voice was undisguised. Jody stroked her shoulders in a touch both sensual and reassuring but, as her breathing gradually returned to normal, Grace began to experience a new sense of excitement and longing and it was the turn of her own hands to slide downwards, drawn inexorably by the knowledge of the heat and enchantment that she knew was waiting.

Her fingers discovered the tawny thatch that was wet from her own passion and Jody moaned softly and her hips moved to meet the diffidently exploring hand. Grace's fingers explored the voluptuous liquid heat and she felt a corresponding wetness flood her own body yet again. Her mouth was suddenly salivating and the longing, whose focus she now understood, could not be denied despite her nervousness. She left the haven of the silken breasts, slid down between Jody's legs and pushed them apart. Her action exposed the pink flower within and with utmost awe and tenderness her tongue caressed first the petals then the fragile bud at its heart. Jody's sigh and the faint flutter of her stomach muscles spurred Grace's excitement and her mouth began an intuitive rhythmical adoration of this most beautiful, sweet but salty bloom.

As her tongue and lips moved, so Grace's hands also moved, stroking the trembling muscles of the smooth, powerful legs and the velvety roundness of soft but athletic buttocks, until she felt herself to be intoxicated by the unleashed power of this most intimate pleasure. Instinctively Grace followed the cadences hinted at by the intense undulations that began to shake Jody; then, as her breathing became faster and shallower, Jody's legs reflexively spread even wider as if she wanted to absorb Grace's unending kiss.

While her tongue probed and suckled this body she cherished more than any other Grace sensed an even deeper chasm of craving unfolding and, reckless but instinctively sure, her searching fingers entered and spontaneously found the mysterious rhythm within. As Jody began to whimper her rising desire, Grace's awareness of her internal tempo became ever more heightened as she took her cue from the slowly rising pitch of Jody's moans.

"I can't . . . I can't . . ." Jody whispered frantically but then, at Grace's tender insistence, she could.

* * * * *

Grace and Jody lay tangled together beside the still green water of the billabong. Neither moved for long, languorous minutes as they savored the unique and new feelings each had wrought in the other. Then Jody lazily turned and kissed Grace and shyly asked, "Is that what I taste like?"

Grace ran her tongue slowly around her lips and nodded. "You do." Then she opened her eyes wide. "Hey! Hold on a minute. I thought I was supposed to be the virgin! Hasn't anyone done that to you before?"

Jody looked sheepish and grinned. "Nobody who I've ever kissed afterwards," she said ruefully. They watched a flight of parrots zip and wheel around the treetops for a few minutes while each privately considered this revelation. What neither was yet prepared to admit was that their lovemaking was like nothing either had ever experienced before. For Grace, too, there was the specter of Jody's imminent departure; for Jody there was her own knowledge of the impossibility of her lifestyle and her long-held conviction and experience that she and any kind of permanent relationship were incompatible. She tried to put these thoughts away as she drifted in a state of blissful half-awakeness, listening to the birds high above them and feeling the solid thud of Grace's heart beneath her cheek.

The memory of what Grace had just done was vivid. She relived the moment of whitewater white heat rearing up and crashing through the floodgate of long unacknowledged passion, shattering her reserve and control in a pure cry of joy that had echoed around the fastness of the billabong. She had been free and soaring headlong into the kind of orgasm she thought happened only to other people. She shivered.

Grace stroked Jody's long hair and idly wondered how she ever got the reputation for being a weirdo — and also wondered whether Red could possibly be right that she had not had other relationships on the road. It didn't seem possible. And she too shivered as she recalled it.

"Are you chilled?" Jody whispered.

Grace shook her head and raised herself on one elbow so she could look down at Jody. "No, I've never felt so warm," she smiled. "How about you?"

Jody shook her head and sighed happily. "I've ..." She paused and considered for a moment, then she sighed again and said, "I have never felt so good."

Grace's heart somersaulted and she turned her face away quickly to hide the mix of joy and despair she knew must be there. Jody's lovemaking had been so unlike the boring, unsatisfying quasi-sexual encounters of her youth and the crude and vicious acts that she had experienced with Scott that it was almost unbearable to think about. As she watched a beetle scull across the billabong the thought crossed her mind that in this place of her conception she had been reborn as a sexual being. She shivered again and Jody's arms clasped her protectively.

"We'd better be getting back," Jody whispered and Grace was certain there was a hint of regret in her voice.

CHAPTER EIGHT

By the time they got back to the roadhouse, night had fallen. They were late and, Grace suspected, what she had been doing must surely be written in flashing red neon lights all over her face. She parked the truck and switched off the engine and lights. In the silence Jody took her hand and they sat quietly for a minute more, then they climbed out and prepared to face the world again.

Grace was desperately thankful that it was her nominal "night off" and that she did not have to immediately face the bright lights and inquiring faces of her parents and the locals. She decided to try to be light-hearted as she gathered up her untouched painting gear. "I'd offer you a trip to the movies," she said to Jody, "but we'd have to drive about four hundred miles. Or I could offer you a good dinner in a roadhouse not too far from here."

Jody took her hand and raised it to her lips. "I'll take the dinner," she said. "And then I'd like to invite you to my place for a nightcap."

Grace laughed. "Done. I'll see you in the kitchen in about twenty minutes. I should have warned you first that it will be my cooking and not my mother's, but I'm afraid I was feeling unscrupulous."

"I'll remember that."

Reluctantly Grace backed away and then made for the welcoming sanctuary of her cabin. Standing once again under the fierce jet of the shower, she felt the parts of her body so long unused and unexercised now tingling and tender. And there were also little pains and feelings that she knew had never been present in her life before. She knew, even without recourse to conscious thought, that she was in love with Jody with a depth and passion that she would not have believed was possible. She found herself smiling and experiencing the kind of deep-seated contentment that she had often observed on her mother's face, but had never anticipated feeling herself. Yet she was also aware that she had committed the classic foolish act of falling for the visiting star, and as the water stung her willing flesh, she tried desperately hard not to think about what would happen when Ol' Tammy was back on the road and taking away Jody from her.

* * * * *

Jody stopped in the doorway, taking in the scene of ebullient domesticity and her heart lurched with longing for its warmth and ordinariness. The big table was set with six places and Iris and Ed were already deep in conversation about the possibility of getting good Italian food in Texas. She quickly picked up that Iris had invited herself along on their American tour and the two seemed to be thoroughly enjoying their fantasy. Grace's father was uncorking wine bottles and humming happily and his wife was polishing fine stemmed wine glasses with a soft white cloth.

At the gas range, Grace was concentrating on a pan of bubbling sauce, carefully sniffing the steam that rose from it as she tipped in splashes of white wine. She occasionally stirred a bubbling pan of arborio rice with a long-handled wooden spoon and Jody watched the ripple of the muscles of her back and arms with a pleasure so intense it was breathtaking. In a plain red T-shirt and faded blue jeans, Grace was a picture of boyish practicality, except that there was nothing boyish about the swell of her breasts and the curve of her waist and hips, which were built in the same proportion of firm flesh and taut muscle as her arms and shoulders. She was strong and womanly — it was an intoxicating combination and Jody was quite dizzy with it.

"*Buona sera*, Jody!" Her light-headed reverie was over in an instant as Tony spotted her clinging weakly to the door. "Come in, come in!" He kissed her heartily on both cheeks and led her to the table, where she was similarly greeted by Iris and Margaret, while Ed watched and smiled and Grace simply looked at her with eyes that made her heart soar.

"Can I do anything to help?" she asked, feeling anything but helpful.

Grace smiled and shook her head. "Just keep them under control, if you don't mind and dinner will be about five minutes."

"Here, Jody, give Grace a glass of wine." Tony passed Jody a glass and she gratefully took the opportunity to move closer to Grace and hold the glass while Grace finished flipping the last of a batch of chicken fillets. Then she took the glass and their fingers overlapped for a moment longer than was necessary while Jody's heart beat painfully.

"This isn't exactly the quiet dinner I had in mind," said Grace ruefully, "but it will taste good."

"This is a perfect dinner," Jody said quietly. "I can't think of anywhere I'd rather be, or people I'd rather be with. And I know I will have you all to myself later." She turned away quickly before Grace's proximity became too much like a magnet to an iron filing and returned to the table where Iris promptly jilted Ed and turned her full flirtatious attention on Jody.

"Tell me about America, Jo-dee," she said, patting the chair beside her. "Tell me about the skyscrapes and the murderers and the drugs."

"Oh, Iris." Jody groaned. "I'm so sorry, but there aren't any 'skyscrapes' where I come from." She sat in the chair and slumped her face comically in her hands. Then she sat up and said brightly, "But there are murderers occasionally and I think there are quite a lot of drugs too." She assumed another gloomy expression. "But I don't know much about them. Ask Ed, he knows all about drugs — and bad women."

When the laughter subsided, Iris took Jody's hand in her own and gave it a shake. "You are bad woman, Jo-dee, you are pulling the legs off old woman who has never been to America. Now you tell me about where you come from and no tricks or I give you big smack!"

Jody patted Iris's hand and tried to look solemn. "I promise I will not pull your legs off, Iris. Scout's honor."

Iris still looked suspicious, especially as the others continued to chuckle, but she nodded and waved her hand for Jody to continue.

"Well, ma'am, I come from Washington State, that's in the Pacific Northwest — just across the ocean from Australia, which makes us practically neighbors — and I was brought up in a tiny place called Cannon Beach. It's right on the Pacific and just to the south is a great rock which is very beautiful — not like your big rock, but a nice rock — and there are lots of tourists in the summer and it's quiet in winter. The beach is long and empty although the ocean is pretty much always cold and I lived with my mom in a nice little house just out of town. My dad took off when I was small and I don't really remember him and my mom worked in summer and did what she could in winter to keep us fed and clothed. And that's about it. I started singing in the shopping mall when I was about ten and I won a talent contest one summer, but I didn't really start singing seriously until I finished school. We couldn't afford college and I wanted to start getting professional. So that's what I did and I've been working ever since, getting a little bit better every year and making it a little bit farther up the mountain."

"Hmm." Iris considered this for a moment, then she fixed Jody with a steady eye. "Why you no get married? You plenty old enough."

There was a sudden silence broken by Margaret's "Mama!"

But Jody laid her hand reassuringly on Margaret's arm and grinned at Iris. "I'm not the marrying kind," she said easily. "I never figured on settling down exactly that way."

Iris nodded and pursed her lips in an expression of vague puzzlement. "So the stuff in the papers is true, yes?" There was a clang from the stove as Grace dropped a ladle, but Iris went on calmly, "So how come you don' have girlfriend? You seem pretty nice girl, how come you all by yourself?"

This time even Jody was startled and she gazed at Iris open-mouthed for a moment as the rest of the group around the table gazed at her. Then, as laughter began to bubble up in her throat, her mind clicked back into gear and she said, "Well, would you like to be waiting at home, doing embroidery or something, or living out of a suitcase for ten months of the year, Iris? It's no fit life for a nice girl."

Iris pursed her lips again and shook her head. "Then you must meet wrong sort girl. A good girl who love you would do what it needs. When Alphonse and me first come to Australie, we have no money, he take a job — he drive truck, I see him whenever he get home. Sometime I think he go for two weeks, he come home after seven, eight. Then he find this place, I see in his eyes that we will come here. So we do and here we stay." She looked at Jody's serious face and began to laugh, throwing her head back and clutching Jody's hand before lowering her eyelashes coquettishly and stroking the back of the firm brown hand that held hers. "So Jo-dee! You need find girl like me!"

And this time the laughter rippled and roared around the table and Jody could not look at Grace for the pain that grabbed at her heart. And Grace also avoided looking at Jody, which meant that she saw her father's grim expression, Jody guessed. There was no laughter to break up his tight face. And her heart sank into her boots and hit rock-bottom despite the warmth and fun that surrounded her.

The rest of the evening began what would be the pattern of the two that were to follow: dinner cooked by Grace in the kitchen, then the gradual and agonizingly slow wind-down as first Iris, then Ed and Andy took their leave. Finally Grace and Jody could persuade Tony and Iris that they would clear the kitchen, then they too would climb the stairs to their private apartment above the restaurant, leaving Jody and Grace to finish up.

It was a domestic ritual that they played out with unspoken but passionate need to share this time of ordinariness — despite the almost unendurable hours with the rest of the household. They washed and polished the steel and copper pots and pans, sluiced the floor and cleaned the surfaces, sometimes talking, more often savoring the new experience of an intimate but electrically charged silence. Occasionally their paths would cross and be marked by a fleeting kiss or touch. Once the room was ready for the next morning, they would quietly let themselves out into the night and walk across the yard to Grace's cabin.

The first night Grace could barely wait to close the door before she turned into Jody's arms and began to hungrily reclaim the shapes and sensations that she had discovered just hours ago.

Jody had laughed and held her off. "Hey," she said. "Didn't you have enough dinner?" But then she saw the stricken look in Grace's eyes and she pulled her into an embrace. "Sweetheart," she said softly, kissing her forehead reassuringly. "I'm only teasing, I'm sorry . . ."

Grace shook her head sheepishly. "I'm sorry," she said. "It's just that I've been watching my own grandmother flirting with you all evening and practically offering to marry you. I guess it was all a bit . . ." She shrugged and regarded Jody with honest eyes. "I don't know, I — I really really want you, so much, and I am not very good at being cool about it."

Jody shook her head and held her tight. "It's not cool to pretend you don't care, sweetheart. I've had a lovely evening but I've been hanging out to be with you like this and to kiss you here . . . and here . . . and take your T-shirt off like this and put my arms around you like that and feel you against me like this and . . . have your hands inside my shirt and, oh God, to have you hold me right there so I'm anchored to you and can't move . . . ah, Grace, I want this so badly it hurts."

"So let me kiss it better," Grace murmured and

led her to the bed. There she sank to her knees in front of Jody and with a confidence that astounded her, popped the buttons of Jody's jeans in one continuous movement. She pulled aside the silk shorts beneath the jeans and parted Jody's legs. "Let me, Jody, let me," she whispered as Jody tried to pull her away, whimpering a half-hearted protest. "Let me in," she whispered and her tongue gently but inexorably began its quest for the inner secrets of honey and salt. And, when Jody finally cried out, Grace held her and stroked her quivering body until her breathing slowed and she turned and curled, childlike, into Grace's embrace and slept. Grace kissed her head and whispered, "I love you," into the thickness of Jody's shaggy blond hair, knowing that she was the only one who could hear those treacherous words.

The second morning, Jody awoke to the sounds of magpies caroling and gossiping in the pepper tree that shaded the cabin. In her mind there was a memory of impossible sweetness and gentle pleasure and within her body were the bruises of immeasurable passion and insistent demands. She stretched and then turned toward Grace whose curved form she could just make out in the gray dawn light. She laid her hand gently on Grace's leg, not wanting to disturb her, and carefully examined the rare sensation of waking beside another human being. Instead of the regret and vague embarrassment she had experienced in the past, she felt something that she suspected was happiness, and something else that felt suspiciously like contentment.

As the magpies chattered away and the gray gave way to color, Jody let her mind drift in and out of thoughts and memories. She remembered similarly peaceful mornings waking up in the little house in the sand dunes south of Cannon Beach, when she could hear her mother singing in the kitchen and knew it to be one of the uncommon times when she was not worried about money or the next job. She imagined taking Grace there — driving down from Seattle, showing her the coast and maybe the Olympic mountains, if they would oblige and let their veils of cloud drop. In its rain-drenched greenery it was a part of the world so different from this one, and yet there was something about its silent spaces and untouched fastnesses that made her feel comparably at ease, where cities left her restless and melancholy. Grace stirred beneath her hand and moved slightly closer to Jody. "Mom," Jody imagined herself saying, "Mom, I want you to meet Grace."

She lay back and closed her eyes, recalling the time she had taken home the girl she had thought was the love of her life. Jody smiled wryly at the memory. Eighteen years old and convinced that her mother would understand and adore Louise as much as she did.

While Louise was watching television which, Jody recalled, was what she did most of the time when she wasn't playing keyboards and smoking dope, Kathy Johnson had taken her daughter out onto the deck and they sat watching the sun go down while Kathy smoked one of her two daily cigarettes.

"Mom," Jody said, staring out at the blue-black Pacific rollers. "Louise and I —" She stopped then and hoped that her mother might fill in the blanks, but Kathy waited and smoked her cigarette a lot more assiduously than usual. Finally Jody stuck out her chin and said, "Mom, Louise is my girlfriend. I'm gay, Mom."

After a long moment Kathy sighed and carefully put out her cigarette. "I suppose it would be silly to ask you where I went wrong?" she finally said.

Jody put her hand on her mother's, shocked at the weariness in her voice. "You haven't done anything wrong, Mom. I think I've always been this way. It's . . . natural for me."

Kathy chuckled softly and squeezed her daughter's hand. "Jody, if I live to be a hundred years old I swear you will still be able to surprise me." She put her arm around Jody's shoulders, "I'm not surprised you're gay, my love. I think I've known that a long time, but it's just the way you can say things that are so logical and so unusual, like 'It's natural for me,' and sometimes I wonder which of us has the old head around here. And you're so bright and clever and I'm —" She shrugged and Jody hugged her fiercely.

"You are bright and clever and a wonderful mom," she whispered into her shoulder. "I would be a no-account two-bit fool if it weren't for you."

"Well, my love," her mother said skeptically, "I have to say I think you're a no-account two-bit fool if you think you're going to marry that Louise, but you have to do what makes you happy and — whatever — I'll be right behind you." She paused for one perfectly timed dramatic moment before concluding, "Even if you are being a total lamebrain."

Louise heard their laughter and dragged herself away from the TV set long enough to investigate. But it was even then too late. Kathy Johnson's attitude to Jody's declaration had acted like the switching on of a powerful spotlight and suddenly, to Jody, Louise was no longer a languidly exciting somewhat older woman but a dope-fuzzy bore. She had left the next day and expressed no regrets. When Jody had sat alone on the deck that evening she wept, but only for her own gullibility and youth. And now, she let her hand traverse the length of Grace's shapely thigh, to come to rest at her waist where the concave configuration between hip bone and belly begged to be kissed. For the first time in more than ten years she felt that impulse — to take her lover to meet her mother. But it was all too late.

"I want you to be happy, my love," her mother had whispered as she lay dying of the cancers that had destroyed her once-strong body. "I so want you to be happy." And she had squeezed Jody's hand and, within the hour, was gone.

In an instant, tears flooded Jody's eyes and a sob escaped her throat. She felt Grace stiffen beneath her hand and tried to be silent, but it was too late. Grace turned and her eyes were wide awake and grave.

"What is it?" she whispered, her fingers touching the tear tracks on the splanes of Jody's cheeks. "What's the matter, my love?"

If Grace had not used those words Jody may well have hung on to her composure, but the sound of Grace's voice — soft and overflowing with concern — and the familiar endearment, tipped the balance, and Jody's long-silenced grief and loneliness began to pour out in floods of mourning that threatened to tear her apart. Grace made no attempt to stop her but instead, held her in the tenderest embrace, rocking her and stroking her hair and letting her cry herself out.

As Jody cried, Grace found her own thoughts turning to the future. Before Jody had happened along she had not even begun to consider what might lie ahead for her, so busy had she been putting the past behind and concentrating on regaining some sense of herself that was not battered and fearful. In spare moments her father's health had allowed her to put further thoughts away — no point wondering what she would do when it seemed to be her clear duty to stay and help. Not only her clear duty, but a safe haven, she had to admit. One where she did not have to take any responsibility for personal choices because they were the ones she was able to put aside. Until Jody.

Grace combed her fingers hypnotically through strand upon strand of Jody's hair in a way that she knew would gradually calm the racking sobs that shook the long body. But as Jody's weeping began to subside her own unease and sense of foreboding grew. The time was swiftly approaching, she knew, when their holiday romance — for that was what it was — would have to be put away in a special place with other precious souvenirs when real life was once again upon them. And the aspects of real life that loomed were enough to make her shiver.

On the one hand, Grace's remembrance of the grim look on her father's face hung like Nemesis in the far shadows of her mind, while on the other was her knowledge of the exciting lifestyle and career that lay ahead for Jody which, she was sure, had no place in it for a very ordinary Australian divorcee.

You knew what you were getting into, she told herself. And you know you will have to get yourself out of it.

They were sensible thoughts, but not very comforting. She turned physically and mentally away from the bleak morning light that signaled the rest of her life and forced herself into the present. Jody's cheeks were still tear-streaked.

"Sweetheart," she whispered, "you want to tell me what that was about?"

Jody caressed Grace's face, then she sat up. "I have to find a tissue." She sniffed, scraping her knuckles across her eyes. Grace reached for the box on her bedside table and handed it over. Jody pulled wads from the box and blew noisily, like a child, shuddering with the sadness that clearly still filled her. She sat for a moment and took several deep breaths, then turned back to Grace, her eyes over-flowing with pain.

"My mom," she said in a shaky voice. "I suddenly got to thinking about my mom. She died four years ago and sometimes it feels like it was just yesterday. I'm sorry." Her eyes filled with tears again and she returned to Grace's outstretched arms.

"Jody, Jody." Grace's embrace was all-enveloping and her voice was like balm to Jody's bruised and aching heart. "I'm sure in some ways it will always be like yesterday," she said softly. "We are wrong when we think we get over a great loss. That somehow it gets fixed and that's that. It doesn't get fixed. We just learn to live with it a little better as time goes by. Yet there will always be times when it will strike you so hard you'll fall down for a while." She stroked Jody's hot forehead with soothing fingers. "But that has its sunny side too, sweetheart, because it means your mama will always be with you. Those painful times when you remember her dying will soon be outweighed by the ones when you remember her alive and with you — if you let them."

After a long moment's consideration Jody's answer was a hug so fierce it almost took Grace's breath away.

"You're an extraordinary woman, Grace," she muttered, her mouth against Grace's throat. "A truly extraordinary woman." She closed her eyes and finally said, "I will write to you, Grace." And her words were like a stab to Grace's heart.

That afternoon they drove to their favorite hideaway, on the billabong below Billaluna homestead, and without words, naturally headed for their own spots to work. While Grace drew and painted and made notes, Jody sat some distance away on the smooth bole of a fallen gum tree. For a split second, that morning, she had teetered on the brink of impulse: of asking the impossible — that Grace give up her family, her work and her country for the uncertainties of life on foreign soil, in the alien environment of the music world, where Grace had no experience of the hard grind of touring and recording and where she would be forever waiting, in the shadows, one step behind Jody. She had glanced up at Grace's proudly beautiful profile and swallowed her words. She could not risk it. Could not risk the pain and torment to them both that would surely follow such a precipitate leap in the dark. Resolutely, she put the idea behind her. After a while she began scribbling in a notebook, sucking the end of her pencil and trying out different chord progressions and snatches of melody on her guitar.

It was an afternoon of joyous closeness and one that would prove to be exceptionally prolific. As the light began to fade, Grace packed her gear away with slow fingers and a heavy heart, knowing that each action was a series of "last times." Finally she stood at Jody's feet and said quietly, "We'd better get going, Jody. I think Mama wants to do something a bit special for your last evening."

While Jody's departure was inevitable, Grace was still devastated by the power of the grief that began to enfold her. That evening, as she sat down at the family table in the kitchen with Jody, Margaret and Tony, Iris, Ed and Andy for what had so quickly become the comfortable and familiar end to their day, she could barely speak and certainly could not join in the banter and laughter that batted back and forth around the group. In one bleak, black-and-white moment she caught the concerned eyes of Ed and Andy upon her and forced herself to smile, but the effort was physically painful and she felt as if her face and heart would break.

She knew that she had no claim on Jody — into her mind flashed Jody's grave face as she had spoken in the small hours of the previous night. "You know I have to leave, Grace." She had glanced fearfully at her lover, almost as if expecting the worst.

In a light voice that she had dredged from she knew not where, Grace had reassured her, "We made no promises, Jody. The only sure thing about your arriving here was that you would leave. And when you do I will get a good night's sleep and maybe get some work done." Her smile had cost her dearly, but it was enough to see the apprehension fade from Jody's eyes.

She was grateful at least that Jody had been straightforward and honest about her life on the road being the reason why she always avoided involvements. It had been easier for Grace to accept that than simply that she had been an interlude.

"The rock 'n' roll life is no basis for commitment to relationships," Jody had mused on one occasion when Grace had asked her about life on the road. "I've seen too many sordid break-ups when loved ones left behind go elsewhere for comfort, and watching love turn to hate is not something I'd like to risk again."

Grace understood only too well the sense of being burned by such events, so her pride would never allow her to argue anything different. Nevertheless, as she had lain in Jody's arms in the early hours of the morning her heart was heavier than it had ever been and she could not stop the tears.

It was only when she reached up to touch the face she had come to love that she found it wet and Jody finally said, "It's going to break my heart to leave you, Grace."

"I know," Grace said and held her tight. And

even as Jody kissed her roughly and desperately as
never before, Grace could not understand why she did
not simply say to her, "Come with me." If she did,
Grace knew she would follow her to the ends of the
earth. But Jody did not and all too soon, the sky
turned to gray and a magpie began singing.

CHAPTER NINE

Before climbing up Ol' Tammy's steps Jody kissed Margaret on both cheeks, shook hands with a subdued Tony, gave the eternally grateful Jenny a smothering hug and then stopped in front of Grace. She placed her hand on her heart and tried to grin. "You showed me some very special places, Grace," she said warmly. She leaned forward to kiss her but the pain in Grace's heart was close to unbearable and she turned so that Jody's lips made contact with her cheek. "Whenever I think of them and you my heart will be on fire."

"Maybe it's just indigestion," Grace joked in a tear-strangled voice. "All this rich Italian food."

Jody tried to laugh but it didn't work too well. "I'll write."

Grace shook her head. "You'll be busy. A postcard from the Alice would be nice." She did not dare look up, nor into Jody's eyes, but instead stared at the tips of her black boots until her eyes blurred.

"Sure, okay." Jody turned abruptly and disappeared into the bus, the hydraulic door hissed closed and even as Grace struggled to swallow the sobs that rose unbidden and unwanted in her throat, Ol' Tammy was a cloud of dust.

Grace made it to her cabin before the despair that had been threatening to choke her broke through the dam of her determination. An hour later, as the tears began to subside, her mother softly entered the cabin with two glasses of cognac.

"I think we need this," she said sadly to her daughter. "And then we may have another one." She brandished the bottle that had been clutched beneath one arm.

Grace laughed and cried as she engulfed her mother in a bone-crunching hug of pure despair and grateful affection. "Oh, Mama," she said helplessly.

"I know, sweetheart, I know," Margaret said and Grace could hear the tears in her voice as she stroked Grace's head. In time, even Grace had no more tears left to weep and with her mother's help, she began to slowly and painfully pull together the shattered pieces of herself.

"There is nothing like good cognac," Margaret said as she poured herself a second. "Every time I get angry with the French I have to forgive them for their cognac and champagne."

Grace grinned and downed the remains of her own golden brown restorative. "When do you get angry with the French, Mama?"

"Quite often my darling, I am Italian and they — they are French!" The two women laughed and Margaret poured more cognac into Grace's glass. "Drink up, my darling. I don't think there is any more of this until the brewery truck comes. Your father is going to be furious."

Grace sighed. "I think my father is furious anyway, Mama," she said sadly.

Margaret shrugged. "He is a man. Men get furious about things they don't understand."

"And you, Mama? Doesn't it make you furious?" Grace asked hesitantly.

"I am sad that you are unhappy. I am sad that the course of your life is not turning out to be an easy one. I was furious that marriage to Scott did such terrible things to you. That made me furious. Now, I am just very very sad. And I will pray that you get over . . . all this . . . very soon."

Grace frowned and hesitated before continuing, "Mama, do you know why I'm sad?"

"You are more than sad, my darling. I think perhaps what happened to you with Scott has made you vulnerable to —" she pursed her lips. "To somebody who is maybe gentle and not like your husband. But you will get over this craziness. You have just been on your own too long and Jody — well, I expect she is very experienced at this kind of thing. You know — seducing defenseless girls."

123

Grace spluttered, shook her head violently and swallowed another burning mouthful of cognac. "No, Mama, I can't let you think that. That's not fair. You might not like to know this but Jody didn't try to seduce me. It was the other way around."

Margaret said nothing as she swirled the cognac around her glass. Finally she looked up and sighed sadly. "I knew it," she said heavily. "I did not want to admit it, but I knew it. I blame myself. I threw you together. I thought it would be good for you to be with someone your own age for a change. I thought it would take you out of yourself." She shook her head and her eyes were hard. "The blessed saints know that I did not think it would make you lose your mind. This madness must be some delayed reaction to what happened with Scott. Perhaps you should see somebody about it — get help."

Grace sighed; her heart was threatening to sink even further than it had already dropped. Finally she sat up straight and looked square into her mother's eyes. "Ma, please listen to me. I love Jody and she's gone. I knew she would go. I tried not to love her. I did not expect to love her. Nothing like this has ever happened to me before, but I know I love her." She continued to regard her mother steadily. "I'm sorry to do this to you, Mama, and I expect it will pass in time, but I do love her."

"Why did you not go with her?" Margaret asked quietly. She looked defeated.

Grace shrugged helplessly. "She didn't ask me to."

Margaret sighed and rolled her eyes. "You learn nothing from before? You have no choice in this?"

Grace shook her head. "I just couldn't, Mama. She said right at the start that she doesn't get involved. She was honest. It's my fault that I feel this way."

Margaret looked astounded. "Grace, I saw the way she looked at you the day she walked into the restaurant, although I did not believe it. And you —" She looked into her brandy glass for inspiration. "My darling, I cannot believe that you two could be so foolish. Or perhaps it is prideful. Were you too proud to . . . to show your feelings?"

Grace shook her head in anguish. "How could I, Ma? It would have seemed like I was trying to trap her — to get something out of her. People must do that all the time. I couldn't, Mama. I just couldn't."

Margaret sighed again and nodded, reluctantly understanding her daughter's dilemma. "You remember when I told you off for your prejudice?"

Grace nodded and grinned. "And you were right."

"Perhaps, but I was a hypocrite too, because when I put two and two together and began to realize what was happening, even though I could not admit it to myself, I have to admit I was not happy. How could I be? I want beautiful grandchildren and a marvelous son-in-law . . . but . . ." She stopped speaking and took Grace's hand and they sat in silence for a while, then Margaret said, "I would like it if your life was not difficult. I want you to find somebody who will love you as much as you deserve. Marrying a man is no guarantee that your life will not be difficult, nor that he will love you — I have thought this through and I believe it. But to make your life with Jody, if that is what you want, is to take a path of such difficulty and unhappiness — not just for you, but for your family — that I cannot hope it will happen. I am being very honest with you."

Despite her grief, Grace hugged her mother. "Mama, I appreciate your honesty and I understand how you feel. But whatever happens in my life," she swallowed hard, "it will not be with Jody."

Two weeks later, when Grace was just about able to get through a day without falling into a black hole of depression, a postcard arrived from Alice Springs. *Alice Springs was Alice Springs,* it said in Jody's straight up and down hand. *Filming was endless but went well. I'm writing a lot. I miss you. Jody.*

Grace read it several times over and every which way, searching for hidden meanings. She was forced to concede that all meaning was contained in those nineteen words and that there was nothing symbolic in the picture — a lurid depiction of the town's backdrop of the Macdonnell Range at sunset. It was a postcard, she told herself, just a postcard — from a friend. Then she turned to the other envelope bearing her name. At its top left-hand corner was the coat of arms and address of her old university and department.

"Who's that from?" her father asked, his curiosity uncontainable. Its sender had written in his name by hand.

"Cameron Gardner, my old professor," Grace had replied. His handwriting was like his signature — diffident and graceful — but his intention was plain enough. He had secured funding for a three-month habitat-mapping trip to Macquarie Harbour on the west coast of Tasmania to research the falling population of an unusual fish eagle. He wanted Grace to be on the team and, like everything else he did, he wanted to do it yesterday.

Grace read the letter twice, savoring the pleasure of being sought after for such a project and feeling the bubbles of fright and anticipation rising and bursting in her stomach. But there was also another feeling — an irrational one that wanted to stay close to where she had been with Jody, as if it somehow would keep their love alive.

Grace was mulling over the stupidity of this feeling when she sensed two pairs of eyes boring into her. Margaret and Tony could barely suppress their curiosity and Grace grimaced and handed over the letter. "Sorry," she said. "Here, read it yourselves."

Her father grabbed the letter and read it aloud, his voice beginning to shake with pride as be grasped its contents. Finally he set it down on the kitchen table and beamed at Grace and Margaret. "This is wonderful, Grace! This is what you have been waiting for!"

Grace nodded, still feeling a foolish heaviness in her heart. "It is, Dad. I'm very lucky."

"Lucky! You deserve this, you have put in all the hard work. You deserve it."

"Thank you. But can you manage without me?"

Tony and Margaret looked at each other. Whatever unspoken messages passed between them, it was obvious that as much as they loved their only daughter, they wished her a couple of thousand miles away. And for whatever reasons, Grace did not at that moment care to think about.

The rest of the day passed in a flurry of faxes between Cameron Gardner and the machine in the corner of Davanzo's roadhouse office. It seemed the team really was leaving for the island state imminently and Grace would have to follow them as best she could.

We want to make the best of the time we've got in Tassie, Professor Gardner had written. *You know how variable it can be, so the sooner we get there the better.*

Grace had shown the fax to her mother who nodded, a mixture of relief and sadness in her eyes. "It is for the best, Grace," she had said quietly. "This is a godsend, you know."

Grace could only agree, although, she surmised, for slightly different reasons. Being around the roadhouse, where idle reminiscence and gossip about Jody stabbed her in the heart on a daily basis as the papers reported the progress of the tour and film, was becoming no more bearable with the passage of time. She dreaded the daily newspapers and Iris's excited reading out of every little item about the young woman she insisted on calling "my girlfriend." And although she had even managed to deal in a polite if not exactly amiable way with an RV whose occupants were looking for "where Jody Johnson slept," the amusement value had quickly worn thin.

Longstanding patrons asked her, virtually on a daily basis, to relate the story of when a half-dozen young women had clomped into the restaurant in heavy black work boots, nose rings, tattoos and the worst haircuts in the southern hemisphere. Grace had steeled herself to answer their breathless questions and then taken them out to Jody's cabin. It had occurred to her, in a rare flash of humor, that her directions were not entirely truthful: Jody had spent very little time in the double bed upon which they were perching with great reverence. If she was going to be fair, she would have taken them to her own bed. But, as she told herself afterwards, she was not feeling that fair. And probably never would.

Then Iris had got wind of the fans' visit and her suggestion that they have T-shirts printed up with the design of a plaque and "Jody Johnson Slept Here" was almost a joke too far for her grand-daughter. By the time the third people-mover in a week had rolled in full of pale-skinned young women, all looking for Jody, Grace had left Margaret to show them around, even as she wondered whether it was quite the right thing to do. Their shining eyes and delight at being able to take snapshots of one another outside "Jody's door," however, led her to decide grudgingly that there could be no harm in it. Especially when it meant extra business at what would otherwise have been a quiet time of year.

The evening after the arrival of Cameron Gardner's letter Grace began pulling her field gear out of its storage bag and putting it into waterproof plastic bags for packing. There were sturdy warm shirts, trousers and sweaters, two pairs of water-proof binoculars, a portable studio, three cameras, a custom-made flight bag holding three variously mammoth lenses; and all the other paraphernalia that seemed to be vital in the observation and recording of elusive birds and their habits. Her emotions were in turmoil as she slotted each item into its place in her tough canvas bags. The excitement was un-deniable, especially the sense of justification and satisfaction that her work was being recognized by her peers, but the underlying pain was also un-deniable. Leaving Barralong would now accelerate what she knew, in her heart, she would have to do some day: confront her worst fears and four-in-the-morning misery, that once back on the road and with America beckoning, Jody would be caught up with her old life and have forgotten her truckstop romance.

Grace was right and wrong. The Australian tour and its accompanying filming schedule had passed for Jody in a haze of pain-filled determination. On the road north as they left the roadhouse she had fallen into Ed's arms and cried as he had never seen her cry before. She had no need to explain to him, no need to rationalize her state. He had held her as she fell apart and he held her until she could begin most piteously to put herself back together again. It had taken hours and they had both been grateful for the cavernously empty vehicle and Andy's discretion as he concentrated fiercely on the highway ahead and turned the rearview mirrors so that there was no way *he* could intrude.

Sadly, Ed was soon to realize that there was no way he could intrude either. After the initial storm of grief had passed, Jody put up barriers of bright behavior to hide the damage and flatly refused to let anyone — including Ed — pass.

One crisp early morning, in Alice Springs, they had stood looking out at the red-and-purple-slashed ridge of the Macdonnell Range to the south of the town and Ed said softly, "Until you've been here you wouldn't understand that this is an incredibly beautiful country." Jody turned to him with tears in her eyes and just nodded. He placed his arm around her shoulder and tentatively went on, "And until you've been there you wouldn't understand that it can be incredibly hard to love someone."

Jody said nothing for what seemed like an age, then her shoulders straightened and her chin went up and she said, "She was a really wonderful person, Ed. She made me feel —" She shrugged and frowned. "I don't know, sort of easy with myself, you know?"

He nodded and gave her shoulder a squeeze. "I know," he said. "So why isn't she here?"

Jody shrugged away his hand then and moved away. "Real life isn't like that, Ed. This is not a fairy story with a nice godmother and a happy ending. This is how it is."

And Ed was so dumbfounded he said nothing. The moment passed just as the colors of the early sun striking the vivid ridge of hills had also changed. It was an exchange of intimacy that, it quickly became clear, Jody did not want to repeat.

At first she would eagerly check each morning's faxes and messages but none were ever from Barralong Creek. Once Ed tried to say that Grace was not likely to make contact in such a fashion, but Jody angrily brushed aside his words with a brusque "I don't know what you're talking about." She distanced herself from him physically and mentally in a way that marked a new phase in their relationship. Ed's sadness was compounded by his conviction that what she was doing would cause her nothing but grief.

Then, as the days and weeks rolled by, Jody's iron resolve to get through and perform to the very limits of her talent took over. Forced to the periphery, Ed nevertheless watched over her with a degree of concern that he had not felt in the past. Something about the thin, haunted look gave an edge to her beauty and to her work that had not formerly been present, even after her mother's death. It was an edge that Ed felt they could do without, so dangerously fragile did it seem to make her. Day after day she would look at the itinerary he handed her, ask questions, make sure she understood what was required, then nod her head and start into it. Indomitable, resolute and unstoppable. When the last item on the day's list had been accomplished she would disappear to her hotel room, order room service and — he would later discover — write songs until exhaustion overtook her.

One evening, at the end of the tour, Jody and Ed got dressed up, he in his favorite pale pink tux and she in an elegantly revealing black gown, and took themselves off to sit at a white-draped table in the Sydney Opera House's beautiful restaurant for what Ed had hoped would be a celebration and reconciliation. That Jody felt the same way was evidenced in her agreement to the occasion and the care she had taken in preparing for it. After a dinner that both agreed was memorable and fabulous Jody eventually said, "Grace would love it here."

It was the first time she had mentioned Grace's name and Ed was rendered speechless for a moment. Then he set down his wine glass and said simply, as he had before, "So why isn't she here?"

Jody swirled the rich golden fluid in her glass and held it up to the light so that she did not have to look directly at Ed. "She has her own life. It wouldn't work, Ed," she said in a voice of deathly flatness.

"How do you know? It seemed to work pretty well from where I was standing."

Jody shook her head. "That was like . . . time out. It wasn't real. We both knew that. This kind of life isn't for Grace."

Ed snorted and gestured at the soaring roof and serene surrounds of the harbor beyond the sculpted glass walls. "This isn't Grace's kind of life? The Bennelong isn't Grace's kind of life! Did you ask her?"

"Don't be silly, Ed. You know what I mean. Anyway, I broke my rule and now I'm paying for it. It won't happen again."

"What?" Ed's voice was louder than he anticipated and he winced and sat forward to say, more quietly, "You've said some crazy things in your time, Jody, but that's just plain stupid. Now gimme a break and tell me what you think you mean?" His exasperation was extreme.

Nonplussed, Jody said nothing, but swirled the dessert wine around her glass as if completely fascinated by its color and form.

This time Ed was not to be put off. "Well?" he demanded in a voice gone icy.

She looked at him then, clearly surprised that he was angry. "Well, nothing, Ed. I . . . I had an on-the-road romance. And I don't do that kind of thing. What more do you want me to say?"

"I want you to say an honest word," he said through gritted teeth. "If Grace Davanzo was an on-the-road romance then you and Red Douglas have

133

more in common than I would ever have dreamed in my worst nightmares." He sat back, grim-faced, to better watch the stinging effect of his words.

She said nothing for several minutes, but watched the city night lights of Sydney. Then she turned back to him and said coldly, "So what do you want me to do? Grovel? Apologize?"

Bewildered, he looked at her. "Jody, look who you're talking to. It's me — Ed. Remember?"

Jody's face did not give an inch. "So, okay, I'm a lying hound. I'm a bitch. I shouldn't have led her on. Is that it? Is that your truth?"

He shook his head in despair. "No, honey, I want your truth. And I think your truth is that you love her and you're afraid to admit it."

She stood up abruptly. "I'm going to the restroom," she said stiffly. "Maybe you could get the check. I'm very tired." And she strode away across the restaurant, unaware of the stir in her wake as diners recognized the tall, sophisticated figure and turned to companions to whisper and speculate.

Later that evening, at his wits' end, Ed finally decided to do what he had never done before — interfere. He rang the roadhouse to speak to Grace.

Tony answered, bellowing ebulliently over the familiar sounds of the busy restaurant. "Ed! How you doing? Where you are? America?"

"Sydney!" Ed had yelled back, "Just thought I'd say hello — and maybe say hi to Grace —"

"You missed her," Tony yelled. "She's gone already."

"Gone?"

"To Tasmania. She is on a big research job. It's a wonderful thing for her. We are all very proud. Very happy. Did Jody not tell you? She telephoned yesterday to say hi to Iris."

"Ah, no, she didn't say," said Ed, his head reeling. "But we . . . ah . . . we've been real busy, you know."

"Sure, sure, you showbiz people. We understand."

"Yeah, well. You know how it is. We're flying back to the States in the morning."

"Oh! Exciting. You keep in touch now. You don't forget us, hey!"

Ed smiled at his own reflection in the plate glass window that was all that was between him and the glittering lights of Sydney harbor, twenty-seven floors below. "We won't forget you, Tony. Thanks for everything."

The next morning, hidden behind huge wraparounds and an unusually surly expression, Jody avoided the possibility of intimate moments with Ed. She disappeared behind an eye mask and slept, or pretended to sleep, on the flight back across the Pacific, and despite Ed's gentle steering toward a few days off, she'd gone straight into the recording studio within hours of touchdown at LAX. It was then that he discovered that, somehow or other, amid the stress and strain and misery of the past weeks, she had written some twenty or so songs and, after the first rough run-through when Jody sang them solo to the rest of the band with just her guitar for accompaniment, Ed could sense that they were busting to be recorded.

* * * * *

Each member of the band went home with a cassette tape of Jody's run-through and, within the week, they had regrouped in the studio with music, extra session musicians and the urgent intention of committing the work to disc. The recording period was potent. Jody virtually ate, slept and dreamed music, arrangements, instrumentations and lyrics. She found herself working with an intensity and passion that she had never previously achieved. The buzz in the studio was electric. From the engineers to the musicians — all world-weary professionals — they knew without a doubt they were participating in something very special. This, they all quickly came to believe, was a smash hit album in the making.

In her rare moments alone, most often at four in the morning after a draining eighteen hours in the studio, Jody crashed on her bed and despite her every effort, found her mind adrift in the magic places where she had been with Grace. And try as she might, she could not keep Grace from inhabiting the semi-unconscious state of waking dream world to which her profound exhaustion and unhappiness seemed determined to condemn her. Most often, she would give herself up to reverie, remembering the golden afternoons as magpies gossiped and parrots zipped across the clearing and a world of tranquility and safety had briefly opened up to her.

Unknown to the others, these memories of sanctuary were the inspiration for the songs she had written and so, she could not get away from them. Mixed in with the exhilaration of making the very best music of her career was a degree of pain that was a new and unwelcome experience. Eventually she had to admit to herself that she was deeply and irrevocably in love with Grace and — she now knew — she had blown her chances by walking away so callously.

At the same time, she was professional enough and ambitious enough to know there was nothing she could do until the recording was completed. The pressure to finish it in time was severe. The national launch date and promotional concert tour had already been locked in months before. Jody could feel in her bones that this album was the one that would put her, once and for all, at the very top and she didn't want to spoil its chances.

When the first pressing of the CD and its vividly designed cover booklet was placed in her hand, Jody felt a pang of pain and pleasure. "This is the one," she said to Red Douglas. "This is the one, Red."

"I know, Jody," said the guitarist, for once dropping all his swagger. "I can tell you I've never done work like this. It's been the greatest. And I'll tell you another thing for free, you better go back and get that girl of yours or you won't be writing like this anymore."

Jody was shocked. "What do you mean?" she said, though despite her round-eyed disingenuous stare she knew exactly what he meant.

"Grace," said Red, grinning wolfishly. "You ain't been the same since you said good-bye to her — and you can't fool me. This album is all about her. You can only make one heartbreak record, then they turn sour. So, if you want my advice, do us all a favor and go and get her." Jody's jaw dropped and he laughed and slapped her affectionately on the shoulder. "And," he added, only half-mockingly, "I'll be jealous of you for the rest of my life."

At that point his latest gorgeous blond sashayed in behind the biggest and blackest designer shades that could possibly pass for a desire to be incognito on the part of someone who desperately wanted everybody to look at her.

Red shrugged plaintively. "Well, I'll be jealous, but I'll try and keep my end up. Know what I mean?" He winked, slung an arm around the blond and left Jody to her own sorrowful thoughts.

Later that day Ed had found her, knees tucked under her chin, staring out across the rooftops down the steep and wooded canyon. She smiled as he entered the room, but she felt no joy in it. "How's tricks, Ed?"

"Good, Jody, good. I've just been on the phone to Maxfield Rose. They've come up with a bit of a detour in the launch plans."

His tone caused her to pull her gaze back from the canyon view and frown at him. "Oh really?"

"The advance sales in Australia are through the roof. It'll go platinum there before it hits the stores. And they think a quick in-out, one-gig televised launch in Sydney — at the Opera House — will give the rest of the tour a really hot image to kick off with."

Jody's eyes darkened. "I don't think I want to go back to Australia, right now, Ed. Not even to the Opera House."

He sighed and it was his turn to stare out the window. Then he looked down at her thin face and impulsively placed his arm around her shoulders. "I know she's gone off to some jungle or other," he said gently.

Despite herself, Jody grinned. "Tasmania is not exactly jungle."

"Whatever. Look, we should do this gig, I think. It has a lot going for it." He hesitated, then went on. "And I think you should at least send a CD to Grace, and I also think you should try to get in touch with her — maybe they have talking drums down there, or something. But I think it would be good for you. Sort it out, once and for all, so we can all get on with our lives." And then he left the room and Jody to a new set of jumbled thoughts.

Later that day she pulled down a baseball cap over her distinctive hair, then took the symbolic first disc to the post office, bought a CD carton and slipped in a note that said only, *I hope you like this and maybe recognize it. Please come to the gig at the Sydney Opera House on July 1. I miss you. Jody.* She wrote the address of Davanzo's Roadhouse on the package, sealed it with a kiss, said "What the hell," to neutralize the sentimental gesture, and dropped it into the mailbox.

CHAPTER TEN

The CD traveled almost a third of the way around the globe on its way to Grace. After a week it was in the bag that was dropped off on the counter of the roadhouse. A day later, after much soul-searching and late-night arguing between Tony and Margaret, it was redirected and on its way south. Over Bass Strait the aeroplane hit the turbulent air common in the stormy winter weather of the region and the CD, with the rest of the mail, was tossed around along with the struggling plane. And then it bounced along the winding mountain roads to the heart of the southwestern coast region of the island until it reached Strahan, the fishing village on the great enclosed harbor where the university expedition was based.

That morning, Grace was taking it easy with a hot bath and leisurely breakfast after a week of camping in the wet and mist-drenched depths of a forest three or four miles away across the water. She was feeling almost good again. Her work was progressing and she knew she was doing well. The rest of the team of six were decent men and women she had known — more or less — for several years, and she felt at ease in their company, professionally and personally. The region in which they were working was breathtakingly beautiful, virtually unmapped wilderness and, despite the cold and wet, she was enjoying that too. And then there was Cameron Gardner.

The night before, over dinner at the local French restaurant, her professor had looked deep into her eyes and said, "I don't know why I didn't see you before, Grace. You've changed somehow. You were always lovely and a good student, but now . . . there's something else. You are quite beautiful."

Grace had picked up her wine glass, to give herself time to think and to wait for her heart to stop its sudden lurching. Over the weeks she had been aware that Cameron was regarding her more and more fondly, but she had chosen to tell herself it was because he was pleased his protegé was doing so well. Now she had nowhere to hide.

"You're very kind," she eventually said, attempting to smile at him across the rim of her glass. It was a mistake; the soft light of a small lantern on their table cast his craggily handsome face and shock of silvery-reddish hair in a glow that reminded her of Robert Redford. His blue eyes twinkled and the message in them was clear. "I, er, I'm having a wonderful time on this trip," she said, unable to gather her thoughts for anything more meaningful or sensible. She knew where the conversation was leading and she was unsure that she was ready or willing to go along with it. He had not attempted to reach across the table for her hand, nor had he done anything at which she could possibly take offense. It was, she knew and appreciated, a very careful and old-fashioned courtship, as befitting their relative positions in the hierarchy of the field trip. There was also the well-known scuttlebutt that he was separated from his scientist wife who was, in any event, on her own research project, in Washington.

"Grace, you know I find you very attractive." His voice broke in on her thoughts and forced her back to the present. "I would like to —" He cleared his throat and grinned boyishly. It was disarming in such a distinguished face. "I would like to get to know you better."

Grace felt paralyzed and was intensely grateful that a young waiter chose that moment to clear their plates and inquire about their interest in the dessert menu. It gave Grace the breathing space to gather her wits and when they were alone again, she was able to say in a voice that did not tremble, "I would like to get to know you better too, Cameron. But I need a little more time."

He had nodded and smiled beatifically. "Of course,

please don't explain. It's enough to know ... well, it's enough ..."

Later he walked her back along the harborside to her rented out-of-season holiday cottage. The night was cold, but for once the sky was clear and starry. It was beautiful and Cameron's presence — his deep slow voice relating a story of a long-ago silly misadventure — was hypnotic and appealing. At her door she stopped and deliberately turned toward her escort. "Good night, Cameron," she said and waited as he bent his head and kissed her.

She gave herself up to the kiss to kindle the spark and fire that she knew must come if she was going to be able to go to bed with him. His mouth was firm and strong, his hold on her reassuring in its certainty. His tongue tasted of good wine and explored her own with warm insistence. And as he pressed her body against his, she could feel the hardness in his groin despite their winter coats. The familiarity of his maleness was pleasant and his touch was gentle but ... She broke the kiss and stepped back ... but it was not enough — not yet.

"I have to go, Cameron," she whispered, her breathing heavy simply because she had barely been able to breathe in his grasp.

"Of course." He also stepped back, yet she could see he was reluctant to go.

"Good night, Cameron," she said firmly and unlocked her door, feeling for one fleeting moment a flair of panic. But it was misplaced. He watched her until she was safely inside then turned to go, lifting his hand to his forehead in an ironic salute, leaving her to a restless night. And now, on a dank and rainy morning, just as she was settling in beside the potbelly stove with a second mug of coffee and hot buttered toast, the doorbell rang. She was still in her pajamas and a thick woolly wrap. If it's Cameron, he'd better get used to the sight, she told herself as she headed for the door.

It was not her professor, but the mailman holding a small package clearly bearing U.S. stamps and stickers. "Oh God," said Grace out loud, as her heart skipped in that all-too-familiar, uncontrollable way. It was unnerving even if it was evidence that she could still feel some emotion.

"Only a package, miss," said the mailman reassuringly. "Sign here, please."

Obediently Grace placed her signature beside the penciled cross in his book, took the package and returned to the kitchen and its warmth. She sat down and examined the box, suddenly reluctant to go further. She ran her finger over Jody's distinctive handwriting then laboriously slit open the box. She read the note once and set it to one side, then examined the CD. The design was in the form of a postcard with Jody's beautiful smiling face superimposed on a view of Alice Springs and the Macdonnell Ranges. *Postcard from the Alice* was the title splashed across it and, when she turned it over, there was another view of the red desert with, superimposed upon that, the song titles and, at the bottom of the list, three words in tiny white type: *For Grace Davanzo.*

"I think I'm going to faint," Grace said to the potbelly, which continued to crackle, unperturbed. She stared at the dedication, willing it to reveal more than she could divine. She re-read the note — *Come to the gig . . . Sydney Opera House* — fairly unambiguous. *I miss you.*

Grace frowned. She missed her grandmother, she missed home — yes, she missed Jody — but did it mean more than that?

"I don't know," Grace groaned to the potbelly. "What would I be going for? Another night and then 'thanks very much and goodbye'? I don't think I could bear it, I really don't."

On impulse she picked up the phone and rang Davanzo's. Her father answered and, after a greeting that bordered on perfunctory, called her mother. Before she could think better of it Grace told Margaret of the events of the previous night — and of this morning's bombshell in the mail.

"My darling, if I could help you I would," Margaret said sadly. "If I could stop this hurt and confusion, I would. But I can only think you should go and see her. You have to put it to rest. You can't spend the rest of your life wondering what might have been. You have so much more to offer than that, my darling."

Despite the proximity of the crackling potbelly Grace shivered, then she took a deep breath and nodded. "Okay, I know you're right."

"Will you say anything to your professor?" Margaret's anxiety was palpable, even on the phone.

"Only that I have to go to Sydney," Grace said uncertainly. Explaining to Cameron quite why she was fleeing the island was impossible to imagine. Perhaps one day, when it was in the past and they were either friends — or more — she might tell him the truth about the ghost in her past. For now, an invented family crisis would have to do.

Then a real one loomed as her mother said, "What about your father, Grace? I think you must talk to him. He is hurt that you have withdrawn so much from him."

Grace sighed. "I know, Mama, but . . . how could I talk to him about something that makes him so upset? When I spoke to him just now he was so cold."

"There is nothing I can say, my darling. I know how difficult this is for you. But it has been difficult for him too. You are his little girl still and you are not asking him to accept simple things — which is what most men like." Their laughter was briefly like old times and Grace felt a renewed affection for her tough but practical and loving mother. "You must sort it out one way or another — with both of them — my darling," Margaret said.

"I know, Ma. I know. But what's the news at your end? There's nothing to report here except mist and rain and mist."

"It's pretty cold at night now, but we haven't had any rain for about three weeks. We could do with a drop. Oh! I know, Billaluna's been sold. The old boy must have died and one of the stockmen from Bandjulung came by the other day and told us. Sold to some city type, he says."

Grace's mind was an abrupt whirl of images — of happy childhood times fishing in the billabong with her father; picnics with her grandparents; the idyllic afternoons with Jody. She felt all-too-familiar tears threatening to spill and she took deep breaths to quell them. "I've been going there since I was a little girl," she said to her mother plaintively. "That's awful. I wonder what they'll do with it?"

"Nobody seems to know. Your father says they'll probably run goats or alpacas or ostriches or something like that. Now, just hold on a moment and I'll go and fetch him."

As she waited Grace felt a great sense of irony as she recalled her too-easy wise words to Jody about the mix of sadness and happiness that makes up the past and makes it real. Reluctantly, but with a calmer heart, she squared her shoulders to talk to her father.

Tony Davanzo's voice was tense as he greeted his daughter. "I was practicing on my new computer," he said, by way of a peace offering.

"Can I interrupt, Papa?"

There was a pause, then his voice flooded with tears. "Always, Graziella, always," he said, clearing his throat fiercely. "I'm only playing with this new program anyway. I don't know how I managed before. I love this computer!"

"I remember when we were trying to get you to have a look at computerized records. You told Mama that . . ."

Tony laughed. "I know. I know. I was an old fool. But look at me now. Soon I think I might go on the Internet."

Grace groaned. "Have you told Ma?"

Her father's voice was comical. "Not exactly, but I am sure she will adjust if she thinks it will keep me out of trouble."

Grace had to agree. Then she cleared her throat nervously and took a deep breath. "Papa, I need to talk to you."

"You sound very serious, *cara*," he said gruffly.

"I am, Papa," Grace said, through the thumping

of her heart. "Papa, you know how much I love you and Mama, don't you? And you know I'm more grateful than I've probably ever said for everything you've done for me — and for being able to come home when I most needed to —"

"And we too are grateful, *cara*. We would not have been able to manage after that stupid heart attack. It would have been a terrible strain for your mama — and Iris too. And this is your home, my baby, always your home."

"I know, Papa. It will always be home." She hesitated, then went on. "But I have to make my own way and I know you would want me to." Tony was silent. "I know I made a terrible mistake with Scott, and you never said a word to make me feel bad about it." Tony's snort could have meant any number of things. "So I know you will let me go on making my own decisions, even if you don't always think they're very good ones."

Tony sighed. "Even if I think you are as crazy as your mama, I will always let you do as you wish, *cara*. It just might take me a little while to come around to it."

"Well, I think this might take you a little time to come 'round to, Papa, and I'm truly sorry if it hurts your feelings, or anything else it might make you feel, but you have to know that Jody is coming back to Australia for a short visit and she has asked me to meet her in Sydney." The silence was now profound. Grace plunged on, knowing that if she stopped she might never find the words to continue. "Papa, I will understand if you do not approve, but you have to know that..." She stopped, swallowed, took a deep breath and went on, "You have to know that I love her. And if she wants it, I will go with her to America — or wherever she may be going."

Grace paused, wondering what to say next if her father did not speak. But after a moment he sighed wearily and said, "And if she does not want you?"

A cold hand clutched at Grace's heart, but she shook off the sensation. "I will deal with that when I have to, Papa. Mama thinks . . ."

"Your mama! I told you she is a crazy woman. What is this? She is the one who wants grandchildren. Now she is telling you to throw your life away on . . . on . . ." The telephone crackled and Grace held the receiver away from her ear. "She is turning you into a lesbian!" He spat the word as if it were dirty or poisonous. Grace flinched but said nothing. "Why, *cara*? Why? Is it because that Scott was so terrible? Did I do something wrong when you were a little girl?"

"It has nothing to do with Scott, or you, Papa. You are a wonderful father and I love you very much. I don't hate men, it's more that I love Jody."

His voice contained a glimmer of hope. "So, if . . . she does not want you to go away with her, you will forget her and look for a nice husband, eh? Maybe that professor of yours . . ."

Grace almost laughed. "No, Papa, I don't think so," she said, but it was true, a relationship of some kind with Cameron Gardner was obviously hers for the asking. The feeling that had been growing between them in the past months was more than simple professional admiration. "Cameron is . . ." She paused. Cameron was — what? She couldn't honestly say.

The silence buzzed for what seemed to Grace like

149

eons as her father waited in clear hope for a reprieve from his fears; then she heard her mother's voice. "So, Antonio, you being a jealous papa or an old bigot?"

"What's worse, *cara mia*?" Grace heard him ask his wife. "Let me guess."

"It's worse if you forget Grace is our daughter and that nothing changes that. And it's even worse if you forget how much we want her to be happy and how unhappy she has been." Grace heard the sound of a smacking kiss. "Otherwise you can be a jealous old papa or a foolish old bigot and I won't mind. Just as long as you remember what's important."

Tony's voice was appreciably warmer as he spoke to Grace again. "Sometimes I remember why I married your mother," he told her. "And sometimes, when she calls me 'old' this and 'old' that, I completely forget all over again."

This time, Grace found a chuckle bubbling up inside her. Her mother had diffused and turned the worst of her ordeal away — as she had throughout her life. "Tell Mama thank you, from the bottom of my heart," she whispered. "And thank you, Papa. I know this is difficult for you."

Tony sighed sadly. "Not half as difficult as it may be for you, *cara*. Now you tell that ... that Jody, if she harms a hair on your head, she will have me to deal with. Even if she does sing like an angel."

CHAPTER ELEVEN

The next night, Grace was standing in the guest bedroom of her aunt Grace's house in an eastern suburb of Sydney wondering what might be appropriate to wear to a number-one-selling country singer's concert at the Opera House. It was not the kind of event of which she had any previous experience. With her choice limited by the lack of glamorous outfits in her Tasmanian wardrobe, she quickly settled on her favorite high-heeled, elastic-sided black boots, pale blue jeans and a soft white shirt with loosely flowing sleeves. Over it she slipped on her aunt's black suede, quilted silk-lined jacket to keep out the wintry Sydney winds. Around her neck she clasped her aunt's string of pearls, and in her ears hooked her pearl studs. It would have to do, she decided. It was light-years from the garb that had become her daily uniform in Tasmania where she had left a puzzled Cameron Gardner with excuses she knew had not sounded as plausible as she would have liked. He had insisted on driving her to the airport and had been so solicitous that she had almost told him the truth; but in the end she could not. The foolish precariousness of her quest did not permit it. And now, here she was and she might as well call a cab and get it over with.

Her feeling of "it will have to do," she recognized, had much to do with the oddly mixed sense of fatalism and foreboding that had begun to grow as she stepped on board the plane at Hobart airport only to be told that the flight would be delayed two hours; and it did not dissipate over the rough passage to Sydney. It was a feeling similar to the cold lump of apprehension that she remembered settling in her stomach when she had left her parents for the first time to go away to school, and when she had taken the step to go beyond the experience of her family and attend university, and again when she had walked up the aisle to marry Scott. The ominous portents, she thought, should have warned her that all might not be well, but she had blithely gone ahead — and survived, more or less.

But this was different. This time what was looming ahead of her was a series of unknowns greater and more complex than she had ever faced before. This was not going to be a school year —

neatly divided into terms and holidays. This was not a marriage with all its givens and well-known expectations. In truth she had no idea what it was going to be — a weekend, a week, an occasional trip to somewhere exotic. Or, more likely, a nice way to say a final good-bye.

When she arrived at the Opera House, Grace saw that the crowds were thronging around the concourse of the huge concert hall and her already fragile courage took a dive as she realized her own ticketless state. She wandered up the stairs, stepping over television cables and dodging dazzling lights and groups of excited fans and hatchet-faced ticket scalpers. Her spirits sank even further. It was a big glittery occasion, she saw and there was no way Jody could be expecting her to turn up.

Tentatively she approached a scalper. "I'm only sellin' pairs darlin'," offered the man, enveloping her in a mixture of tobacco and garlic.

"How much is a pair?" asked Grace.

"To you, two-fifty," he said, grinning.

Grace's heart sank; she shook her head and turned away. She began walking back toward the quay, wondering which hotel Jody might be staying at, when a familiar voice shouted her name. It was Red Douglas waving at her from the steps of a huge semi-trailer from which snaked endless colored cables.

"Hey! Gracey!" he yelled. "Princess! Over here!"

Grace was surprised and pleased to see him and she pushed her way through the crowds as quickly as she could. He put out a hand and pulled her up the steps. "Good to see you, girl," he said and gave her what felt like a genuinely affectionate and brotherly hug.

"You too, Red," she said breathlessly as he led her into the cramped confines of the trailer at whose control console sat an over-large, long-haired and bearded man who completely ignored the intrusion.

"They're recording this," he explained. "I've just been checking the sound levels with the maestro here. Does Jody know you've come?"

"No, I didn't know where to get in touch with her. But don't bother her now, please."

"Nah, I don't think I will, not before the gig. She's bad enough anyway. Never seen her like it before. This album's the big one, y'know? Anyway, you gotta ticket?" She shook her head. "Okay. You come in with me then and I'll get you a good spot. You wanna be in front or in the wings?"

"I don't know. I've never done this before, what do you think?"

"Well, out front you'll get a better view — of me especially!" He laughed at her doubtful expression and gave her another hug. "It's okay, Grace, I know when I'm beaten. So come on, let's get you settled."

The noise and flurry of the soaring interior of the Opera House just about matched the hubbub in her own head, Grace thought. Red magically acquired her a good house seat just five rows from the front of the stage.

"You should be okay here, Gracey. And I'll make sure someone fetches you before the end." He leaned down and planted a smacking kiss on her cheek. "Enjoy the show!" He winked and was gone.

By the time the lights went down and the notes

of Jody's theme tune began to flood the auditorium, the atmosphere was dynamic. The audience looked like the widest cross-section of the population Grace could imagine. All colors, ages and states of anticipation. She could not help but get caught up in the mood. Then suddenly, up crashed the lights and the band members were all there in a blaze of brilliance with Jody in the center, dressed · in glittering black with her honey-gold hair gleaming and shimmering as she moved. Grace gasped as if she had been punched in the heart. Jody was so thin — beautiful, almost luminous — but with a haunted look in her eyes, as she grinned and peered out into the darkness beyond the stage, that Grace's resolve to be cool melted. She slumped back in her seat, too stunned to move.

After setting the mood with three old favorites, Jody took the microphone and began to speak. "We're here for the new album, folks," she said. "I don't suppose you've had a chance to buy it yet." She grinned impishly as a roar of voices told her she was wrong, wrong, wrong. "Well, the three of you who haven't got it yet, don't worry. You'll be able to afterwards." She waited until the laughter subsided, then went on. "And now we're gonna do some of my favorite tracks. This one is the title song, called 'Postcard from the Alice'; and it's about being a long way from home and an even longer way from the one you love and an even longer way from being able to tell her that you do."

A chorus of female squeals from the front of the stage was deafening but when the opening chords of Red's guitar soared out over the crowd, Grace felt her heart constrict as Jody's words echoed into the

155

darkness. She barely heard the words of the song, although the tune was familiar — from an afternoon beside a green-glorious pool — she realized, and she could barely take her eyes off Jody's face. Nor could she take her eyes off the strong, long-fingered hands that had played tunes with her body much as they now fluently worked the strings of the gleaming guitar.

Grace was transfixed as song after song poured from the band, all of them speaking of a love gained and carelessly thrown away, of precious days in a dark and empty world; of making love in secret places and remembering them from far away when the hopelessness of jet-age life intervened. Then, eventually, as the lump in her throat was becoming close to unbearable on Jody's behalf, she saw Red sidle up and whisper in Jody's ear. She saw the thin face light up as if from within as Jody put her hands to her eyes to shade them from the blaze of stage lights and peer out across the footlights.

Tentatively Grace raised her hand and waved and the smile that broke across Jody's face was dazzling. Jody raised her hand high and in a gesture Grace knew would always turn her inside out, she placed it on her heart, then she stepped forward and took the microphone.

"This last song is the first single off the album," she said. "You've probably heard it already, which is why it's number one here and back home — for which we thank you." She bowed slightly and paused while the roar of the crowd rocked the building. "You don't know it, but it's helped me realize a dream. It means an awful lot to me and I truly hope it will mean something to you too. It's about the country and how we love it. Whether that's Australia or America or wherever. And it's about how a person can come to signify everything that's wonderful about the place you love and how, in the end, you can't untangle the one from the other — you love them both so much you know your heart will break if you don't have them with you. So, if you're lucky, you scrape together a down payment on the place and then you hope you can persuade the person to put a down payment on you. This song, although you probably wouldn't guess it, is about a place called Billaluna homestead and a woman called Grace Davanzo. It's called 'Heart on Fire.' "

The roar of recognition and appreciation that greeted her introduction and the first bars of the song all but drowned out the musicians and the abruptly out-of-control beating of Grace's heart. And as Jody and Darren united their voices in a chorus that ascended in swirling harmonies, Grace found herself once again listening in stunned recognition to a tune and sentiments whose genesis she had heard picked out on a single acoustic guitar as Jody sat on Grace's bed, naked and beautifully unaware of anything but the sounds in her head.

Grace was lost in a kaleidoscope of memories of their short time together when a meaty hand descended upon her shoulder and tore her away from the past and from the almost mystical comfort of the exquisite harmonies. It was Andy, resplendent in his roadie outfit of black tour T-shirt, huge bunch of keys, mobile phone and backstage pass hanging around his neck. He grinned broadly at her and beckoned to her to follow him.

In a daze, she stumbled up out of her aisle seat

after him, nearly oblivious of the curious and envious glances cast at her. Looking back toward the stage, she was reluctant to take her eyes off Jody in case — in a re-run of an instantaneously resurfaced childhood superstition that she had played whenever her father had driven off to Adelaide — in that split second when she wasn't watching, something terrible might happen and she might never see Jody again. But Andy gently took her arm and yelled in her ear, "Gotta get you backstage before this lot starts stampeding."

Grace nodded and followed him as best as her shaking knees would permit. It was as if, with the impossible dream almost in sight, her fear was even greater than it had been in the unending days and nights of black despair. Her feet felt leaden and the thumping of her heart was close to unbearable. Andy led the way through an almost invisible door at the side of the stage which took them straight into the cavernous area beyond the public domain. Grace had never been behind the scenes in a theater before. The paint and wood-smelling gloom, with its working lights, ropes and hawsers disappearing upward, unpainted walls and fusty black curtains, was surprisingly unglamorous and workmanlike. Here and there inscrutable men, operating all kinds of inscrutable bits of winking, flashing, pulsing electronic equipment, muttered into the mouthpieces of headsets that for some reason they wore over only one ear.

"Mind where you step, Grace," Andy said into her ear, "you could break your neck back here."

Grace squeezed his arm affectionately, understanding that it was his polite way of saying, "Watch where you're going, amateur, or you'll bring the whole show crashing down around our heads." He guided her into a space between two tall openings and she realized she was right in the wings and not more than thirty feet from where Jody and Darren were crooning into a single microphone, their eyes shut as they took the last notes of the song and their harmony to the same stirring and almost unearthly crescendo that Grace recognized from the radio.

As they stepped back from the microphone in a synchronized bow, the audience — invisible to Grace beyond the dazzling lights — erupted in a wall of sound that was tangible and alarming. Jody and the band acknowledged the roaring, stomping, whistling crowd with whoops, endless bows and waves.

"Thank you!" Jody yelled into the mike. "Thank you very much." And each time she spoke a fresh wave of sound came crashing across the lights.

"My God, is it always like this?" Grace yelled in Andy's ear. He nodded and leaned over toward her so that he could shout back with some chance of her hearing, "It was nearly twenty minutes in Philadelphia."

She shook her head in astonishment and then, as the cheering turned to rhythmic foot stamping, she saw Jody and Red consult for a second before Jody turned to the group, gestured "One, two, three, four!" counting with her fist high in the air, and they launched into the pounding opening bars of a final number. A few seconds into it and the audience, Grace could see, was on its feet, and the floor beneath her was shuddering to the beat of two thousand excited fans.

Again, Andy leaned over and cupped his hands

close to Grace's ear. "It'd be better if you went backstage to the dressing room now, Grace. It could get a bit hairy here in a minute when they all come crashing through."

She nodded. "Sure, whatever you think."

He took her arm to lead her past two burly T-shirted men and they bumped straight into Ed, who took one look at Grace and enveloped her in a bear hug, made only slightly difficult by his two mobile phones and notebook computer.

"Grace!" he yelled, lifting her clean off the ground. "How're you doing, girl?"

Grace caught her breath and found herself halfway between laughter and tears. "I'm doing fine, Ed," she said as he whirled her around once again, to the peril of the crew and stage equipment. In the end she was only saved by the trilling of his mobile phone and made good her escape with the ever-solicitous Andy. If only, she thought, if only Jody is even halfway this pleased to see me.

As if he were reading her mind, Andy gave her hand a squeeze and said, "It's really great that you're here, Grace. Really great." The sincerity in his gruff voice again brought tears to her eyes and she hung onto his arm blindly as they negotiated an area at the back of the stage littered with instrument flight cases and other equipment. Then he pushed open a heavily padded soundproof door and they were out of the wall of noise and into a maze of brightly lit corridors, stairs, swinging doors and anonymous doors which opened into dressing rooms.

To her surprise there were almost as many people in the corridor as there were backstage. Some looked like the kind of people Grace expected to see hanging around musicians and some were wearing dogtags around their necks which labeled them "Press." Three groups were fiddling with TV cameras and sound equipment and they were all looking bored. They glanced up disinterestedly as Andy and Grace picked their way past the litter of gear and lounging bodies toward the door at the far end.

"Hey, man, what gives?" said one young man who looked as if he hoped people might think he was from *Rolling Stone*. He peered at Grace from behind heavy black shades, but she doubted he could see very much.

"They'll be down in five," said Andy politely. He pushed on through to a door discreetly labeled "No. 1" and unlocked it with two keys picked from his omnipresent bunch. "In here, Grace," he said softly, shielding her with his bulky body from the belated interest of the media. "Nobody will bother you. Make yourself comfortable and we'll be back in a flash."

Grace reached up and kissed him on his stubbly cheek. "Thanks, Andy," she said sincerely. "You're a pal."

He blushed and rubbed his cheek, grinning as he turned away to be grabbed by a reporter who pointed unashamedly at Grace and said, "Who's she?"

Grace did not wait to hear the answer or its consequences. She closed the door firmly and turned to examine her temporary respite, or prison — which one it was, she was not quite sure. To her surprise, it was not a particularly large or luxurious room. It had no windows, there was a small bathroom to one side through an alcove, a comfortable-looking couch covered in squashy cushions and Jodie's street clothes and, across the room from it, a similarly comfortable and squashy-looking easy chair. Opposite the door was a white-topped counter surmounted by a white light-surrounded mirror. On the counter was scattered the paraphernalia of Jody's stage makeup, a throat spray and throat lozenges, half-empty bottles of spring water, a basket of exotic fruit and, to one side, a picture frame in which were stuck photographs of Grace, taken with and by the members of the band the day they were all leaving Barralong Creek.

To her astonishment she saw there was also one of herself and Jody standing away from the rest. They were laughing at the camera. Jody's arm was about her shoulders and hers was around Jody's waist. She had no memory of it being taken and picked it out of the frame to examine it more closely. On the back was written, in her grandmother's wavering but unmistakable hand, "To my best girl, from Iris Davanzo." Grace sighed and shakily returned the photo to its place.

Since the arrival of the CD her emotions had been on a permanent and violent switchback and she was beginning to feel the effects of being emotionally and physically drained. She sat down in the easy chair and lay back, breathing deeply and trying to unlock the strain in her shoulders. Over the crackling intercom she could hear Jody attempting to convince the audience that this encore would definitely be the last.

This is what life with Jody would be like, Grace thought sardonically. Almost as exciting as waiting around for unpredictable little parrots. It was an unexpectedly comforting thought: that the glamorous life of an international star was actually mostly as mundane as anybody else's. On impulse, Grace hooked Jody's discarded shirt toward her. Without thinking she pressed it to her face and inhaled the familiar scent of her body. Her heart turned over and she closed her eyes. "Please, please make this okay for both of us," she whispered. "Whatever comes out of this, please may we not hurt each other."

Abruptly, the tone of the applause coming over the intercom changed to wild whistling and whooping. A strangely disembodied male TV-announcer-type voice intoned, "Ladies and gentlemen, the Jody Johnson Band." And Grace realized that the band had left the stage for the last time. Within a minute, she could hear the corridor beyond the closed door come alive as the press pack began yelling "Jody! Jody! Just one shot! Here, Jody, this way." Grace got up, meaning to open the door, but then Andy was there, grinning indulgently as he stood back to hold the mob at bay and Jody slipped under his arm and into the room.

Time was suspended and almost ran back on itself as Jody and Grace relived the first moment they had seen each other at Barralong Creek. There was the instant appraisal, the straight up and down of the green eyes and Grace's own wide gaze. Then Jody pushed the door shut, oblivious to the frantic calls and questions behind her. She leaned against it for a moment and in that split second her eyes and face lost the awful haunted look that Grace had seen from the concert hall. She smiled at Grace and it was the same slightly crooked, lazy grin that Grace thought would always turn her heart to butter.

"You're here," Jody said, her voice hoarse. "I didn't know whether you'd come."

Grace held out her arms, to prove her presence, but did not move. "I didn't know whether *you* would," she said.

Jody grimaced and ran her hands through her damp hair and shook herself like a dog. "To be honest, I didn't know whether I would, either," she said. "Is this a good idea, Grace?" She gestured over her shoulder to where they could hear Andy and Ed trying to make some sense of the press gathering. "I have to do a press conference in a minute and then there's a party with a whole bunch of dingbats and hangers-on who think they own a piece of me." She sighed. "Is this a good idea? Do you really want to have anything to do with this?"

Grace's heart sank at the weariness and deep uncertainty she heard in Jody's voice — and saw once again in her face. "Are you asking me whether I want to be a big star and have to do all this stuff?" she asked. "Or are you asking whether I'll hang about while you have to do it?"

Jody shrugged. "Maybe both, maybe neither."

"I didn't come here to play games with you, Jody," said Grace steadily. "You will have to trust me. And I'm going to have to trust you."

Jody stood up, away from the door, and swayed slightly. "I'm tired," she said in a voice that had almost vanished. "I'm so tired, Grace. I thought I could do this without you and I can't. I thought I ought to do it without you and I can't. I thought I wanted to do this without you and I don't." She took a step toward Grace and reached out in supplication. "None of this matters without you. None of it makes sense."

Grace stretched out and took the shaking hand in

both her own. "You don't have to do anything on your own, if you don't want to, my love," she said. "But you have to tell me what you want. I have to know where I stand."

Jody looked puzzled. "What do you mean — what I want? What do you want?" Her fingers gripped Grace's as if never to let go. "What do you want, Grace?"

Grace drew her closer and smiled. "Oh my darling, I want us to be happy. I want you to be happy and I want me to be happy — whatever that takes. I know your life is complicated and demanding and it's probably going to become impossible if this keeps up." She indicated the intercom on the wall where the whooping audience could still be heard, hopeful of yet another encore. "And as for that mob out there in the corridor, I have no idea how to cope with all that. But if you can, I will." She laid her hands on Jody's forearms, her fingers trembling as she felt the smooth flesh she had craved so much.

"Grace," Jody murmured. "You realize that when we open that door and they see you here with me, your life changes forever?"

Grace laid her hands on Jody's shoulders. Her shirt was damp with sweat and it stuck to her back as Grace ran her fingers down its supple length. "My life changed forever the day you walked into it, Jody," she reminded her.

"So will you come with me? Leave Australia?"

"I take it you've bought a chunk of it anyway." She traced the outline of Jody's breasts with her fingers and felt a shudder run through the long body.

"Yes, I bought Billaluna," Jody whispered, her eyes half-closed as she savored Grace's touch. "Since

165

you're half responsible for this album, it was the least I could do. Anyway." She swayed and almost fell against Grace. "I figured it would make it more likely that you might come with me if you had Billaluna to come back to when we want to."

Grace's heart leapt. "You want me with you?"

Jody drew back, a look of shock in the green eyes that were blurry and bruised with tiredness. "Of course I do," she said in bewilderment. "That's what this is all about. I can't live without you, Grace. I love you."

As Grace reached up to kiss her, she tasted and smelled the sharp salt of two hours' hard labor and felt the adrenaline-charged trembling of Jody's body. She could not bear to prolong her confusion a moment longer. "And I adore you, sweetheart," she whispered. "And I'll do whatever it takes for us to be together, if that's what you want." She began unbuttoning Jody's shirt. "And right now, I think a shower and fresh clothes is what it takes."

Jody's hands gripped hers. "You are my lover, not my servant," she said, fright flaring in her eyes.

Grace shook her head and grinned as she bent to lick the salt from Jody's breast. "If I'm your lover, then I think I can take your clothes off if I feel like it," she said firmly. "But you're right. And we'll work all this out as we go along. Including what we're going to say to the press." She unhooked Jody's bra and lifted her breasts free with hands that could not but linger over each one.

"If we're in here much longer, we won't have to tell anybody anything," Jody mumbled dizzily. She reached for Grace's mouth and kissed her in a fierce reclamation of precious territory. But even as she began to fumble the buttons of Grace's shirt the banging on the door intruded.

Grace pulled back. "I think we have to deal with this," she said with difficulty. "They're not going to go away."

Jody groaned and nodded. "You're right. Will you be here with me?"

"Always."

"And I'll always be here with you."

"Then we should be able to make it through."

"Where?"

"Wherever we're going."

Silver Moon Books

Publishers of Lesbian Romance, Detective and Thriller Novels

WILD THINGS, KARIN KALLMAKER
Rich, beautiful Sydney Van Allen is a rising star on the political
horizon. Enter Professor Faith Fitzgerald living under the watchful
gaze of her bigoted parents. Has she the courage to break free
from their stranglehold – and even if she does, what of Sydney's
political career? It seems hopeless; but then love will always find a
way...
(£7.99, ISBN 1 872642 438).

FAIR PLAY, ROSE BEECHEM
Detective Inspector Amanda Valentine returns in a thriller that will
keep you guessing from the first to last page.
(£7.99, ISBN 1 872642 470).

BABY, IT'S COLD, JAYE MAIMAN
The fifth appearance of Robin Miller, this tremendously exciting
thriller lives up to its predecessors.
(£7.99, ISBN 1 872642 403).

DIAMONDS AND RUST, JANE THOMPSON
Author of the very popular *Still Crazy,* Jane Thompson has written
a second novel that lives up to the promise of her first. A poignant
story of a woman who, finally, has to own up to who she *really* is.
(£8.99, ISBN 1 872642 373).

FIRST IMPRESSIONS, KATE CALLOWAY
A stunning debut thriller from exciting new talent Kate Calloway.
(£7.99, 208pp, ISBN 1 872642 381).

DOUBLE BLUFF, CLAIRE MCNAB
Fast becoming the number one lesbian detective writer, Claire
McNab has produced another gripping thriller featuring the
stunning Detective Inspector Carol Ashton.
(£7.99, 190pp, ISBN 1 872642 365).

THE FIRST TIME, eds BARBARA GRIER & CHRISTINE CASSIDY
This collection of lesbian love stories is the fourth in the best
selling series of short story anthologies from Silver Moon Books
(£7.99, 246pp, ISBN 1 872642 357).

SOMEONE TO WATCH, JAYE MAIMAN
Mystery, lust and betrayal are all here in this fourth Robin Miller
mystery from bestseller Jaye Maiman.
(£7.99, 272pp, ISBN 1 872642 349).

DEVOTION, MINDY KAPLAN
A gripping and erotic novel about the dangers of trying to go back
to rewrite history; of risking what is - for what might have been;
and of the power of love over illusion.
(£7.99, 160pp, ISBN 1 872642 330).

PAXTON COURT, DIANE SALVATORE
A wonderful book about how people learn to live together,
overcoming stereotypes and the fear of the unknown. Sexy,
moving and very funny it is this fine author's best book yet.
(£7.99, 240pp, ISBN 1 872642 322).

DEEPLY MYSTERIOUS,
eds KATHERINE FORREST and BARBARA GRIER
Cross the best lesbian mysteries with the hottest lesbian
romances and what do you get? *Deeply Mysterious* Silver Moon's
third collection of lesbian erotic stories.
(£7.99, 304pp, ISBN 1 872642 31 4).

BODY GUARD, CLAIRE McNAB
An unwelcome assignment makes Detective Inspector Carol
Ashton body guard to Maria Strickland - a famous American
feminist under personal threat from the New Right. The only thing
between Maria and her assassin is Carol's courage. Will it be
enough?
(£7.99, 192pp, ISBN 1 872642 306).

SECOND GUESS, ROSE BEECHAM
Amanda Valentine who first appeared in *The Garbage Dump
Murders* makes a welcome return in this compelling thriller.
(£7.99, 208pp, ISBN 1 872642 276).

DESERT OF THE HEART, JANE RULE
Told with all the wit and skill at the command of this fine novelist,
Desert of the Heart stands as a classic of lesbian literature.
(£6.99, 224pp, ISBN 1 872642 21 7).

CONFESSIONS OF A FAILED SOUTHERN LADY,
FLORENCE KING
From her first tentative steps in school, to her college days where
she discovers women in the form of the beautiful Bres, Florence
King's sensationally funny autobiography reads like a novel and is
a treat not to be missed.
(£6.99, 272pp, ISBN 1 872642 23 3).

CAR POOL, KARIN KALLMAKER
Anthea Rossignole is good looking, successful, possessor of a
great house and a fast car. She is comfortable in her closeted world
until she meets Shay Sumoto. A captivating and erotic lesbian
romance from the very popular author of *Paperback Romance.*
(£7.99, 272pp, ISBN 1 872642 24 1).

DIVING DEEPER,
eds KATHERINE V. FORREST and BARBARA GRIER
Silver Moon's second anthology of erotic lesbian short stories
takes over where its predecessor *Diving Deep* left off.
(£6.99, 304pp, ISBN 1 872642 22 5).

CRAZY FOR LOVING, JAYE MAIMAN
Romance and mystery with detective Robin Miller loose in New York.
Jaye Maiman at the top of her form in this sequel to the very popular *I
Left My Heart.*
(£6.99, 320pp, ISBN 1 872642 19 5).

LOVE, ZENA BETH, DIANE SALVATORE
The novel all lesbian America is talking about. The story of Joyce Ecco's
love affair with Zena Beth Frazer, world famous lesbian author. Zena Beth
is sexy, witty, outrageous and recovering from her sensational love affair
with sports superstar Helena Zoe. A passionate novel of love and
jealousy which has the ring of truth.
(£6.99, 224pp, ISBN 1 872642 10 1).

FLASHPOINT, KATHERINE V. FORREST
A contemporary novel in which Katherine V. Forrest brings
together all the skill and passion that have made her the most
popular lesbian author writing today.
(£6.99, 240pp, ISBN 1 872642 29 2).

STILL CRAZY, JANE THOMPSON
A moving and passionate debut novel from an exciting new
lesbian talent.
(£6.99, 176pp, ISBN 1 872642 20 9).

UNDER MY SKIN, JAYE MAIMAN
Following on from the success of *I Left my Heart* and *Crazy for Loving,*
this third book in award-winning Jaye Maiman's highly-charged mystery
series is the best yet.
(£6.99, 285pp, ISBN 1 872642 26 8).

DEAD CERTAIN, CLAIRE MCNAB
Faced with the exposure she has always feared, her integrity and
objectivity questioned as never before, Detective Inspector Carol Ashton
finds her professional and emotional life spinning out of control in this
scorching thriller.
(£6.99, 206pp, ISBN 1 872642 28 4).

SILENT HEART, CLAIRE MCNAB
A moving and erotic love story from the author of the bestselling *Under
the Southern Cross.*
(£6.99, 173pp, ISBN 1 872642 16 0).

UNDER THE SOUTHERN CROSS, CLAIRE McNAB
Claire McNab departs from her famous Detective Inspector Carol Ashton
series to bring her readers this passionate romance set against the
majestic landscape of Australia.
(£6.99, 192pp, ISBN 1 872642 17 9).

I LEFT MY HEART, JAYE MAIMAN
As she follows a trail of mystery from San Francisco down the coast
travel writer and romantic novelist Robin Miller finds
distraction with sexy and enigmatic Cathy. A fast paced and witty thriller
from an exciting new talent.
(£6.99, 303pp, ISBN 1 872642 06 3).

BENEDICTION, DIANE SALVATORE
A wonderful story of growing up and coming out. Its progress through
love, sexuality and friendship will awaken so many
memories for us all.
(£5.99, 260pp, ISBN 1 872642 05 5).

CURIOUS WINE, KATHERINE V. FORREST
An unforgettable novel from bestseller Katherine V. Forrest. Breathtakingly
candid in its romantic eroticism – a love story to
cherish.
(£6.99, 160pp, ISBN 1 872642 02 0).

AN EMERGENCE OF GREEN, KATHERINE V. FORREST
A frank and powerful love story set against the backdrop of Los Angeles,
this passionate novel pulls no punches.
(£6.99, 270pp, ISBN 1 872642 00 4).

Silver Moon Books are available from all good bookshops. However, if
you have difficulty obtaining our titles please write to Silver Moon Books,
68 Charing Cross Road, London WC2H 0BB